Nestled on the rugged Cornish coast is the picturesque town of Penhally. With sandy beaches, breathtaking landscapes and a warm, bustling community—it is the lucky tourist who stumbles upon this little haven.

But now Mills & Boon® Medical Romance™ is giving readers the unique opportunity to visit this fictional coastal town through our brand new twelve-book continuity... You are welcomed to a town where the fishing boats bob up and down in the bay, surfers wait expectantly for the waves, friendly faces line the cobbled streets and romance flutters on the Cornish sea breeze...

We introduce you to Penhally Bay Surgery, where you can meet the team led by caring and commanding Dr Nick Tremayne. Each book will bring you an emotional, tempting romance—from Mediterranean heroes to a sheikh with a guarded heart. There's royal scandal that leads to marriage for a baby's sake, and handsome playboys are tamed by their blushing brides! Top-notch city surgeons win adoring smiles from the community, and little miracle babies will warm your hearts. But that's not all...

With Penhally Bay you get double the reading pleasure... as each book also follows the life of damaged hero Dr Nick Tremayne. His story will pierce your heart—a tale of lost love and the torment of forbidden romance. Dr Nick's unquestionable, unrelenting skill would leave any patient happy in the knowledge that she's in safe hands, and is a testament to the ability and dedication of all the staff at Penhally Bay Surgery. Come in and meet them for yourself...

Dear Reader

When I was asked to kick off the **BRIDES OF PEN-HALLY BAY** series, a very special collection created in celebration of Mills & Boon's centenary in 2008, I was delighted, and also a little daunted. Twelve books, all by a variety of different authors. Twelve fabulous and intriguing plots, all linked together by two central characters. And what interesting characters! Inherently flawed, deeply hurt by their pasts, and interacting with everyone right through the series.

Wow.

One of them, Nick Tremayne, is the father of my heroine, and he has issues—with knobs on!—with the man she loves.

What a challenge! But the characters grabbed me, the community came to life, and I really, really wanted to write their story and introduce you to a charming, cosy, nosy, bustling little fishing port carefully inserted into the Cornish coast a little north of Padstow.

Penhally's a fabulous place. I wish it was real. I'd go and live there in a minute! But Ben and Lucy do live there, the lucky things, and this, for you, is their story. I hope you love them nearly as much as I do.

Caroline

CHRISTMAS EVE BABY

BY
CAROLINE ANDERSON

MILLS & BOON®
Pure reading pleasure

All the characters in this book have no existence outside the imagination of the author, and have no relation whatsoever to anyone bearing the same name or names. They are not even distantly inspired by any individual known or unknown to the author, and all the incidents are pure invention.

First published in Great Britain 2007
Harlequin Mills & Boon Limited,
Eton House, 18-24 Paradise Road, Richmond, Surrey TW9 1SR

© Caroline Anderson 2007

ISBN: 978 0 263 85278 3

Set in Times Roman 10½ on 12¾ pt
03-1207-50337

Printed and bound in Spain
by Litografía Rosés, S.A., Barcelona

Caroline Anderson has the mind of a butterfly. She's been a nurse, a secretary, a teacher, run her own soft-furnishing business, and now she's settled on writing. She says, 'I was looking for that elusive something. I finally realised it was variety, and now I have it in abundance. Every book brings new horizons and new friends, and in between books I have learned to be a juggler. My teacher husband John and I have two beautiful and talented daughters, Sarah and Hannah, umpteen pets, and several acres of Suffolk that nature tries to reclaim every time we turn our backs!' Caroline also writes for the Mills & Boon® Romance series.

Recent titles by this author:

Medical™ Romance
HIS VERY OWN WIFE AND CHILD
A WIFE AND CHILD TO CHERISH
MATERNAL INSTINCT

Mills & Boon® Romance™
CARING FOR HIS BABY
THE TYCOON'S INSTANT FAMILY
A BRIDE WORTH WAITING FOR

BRIDES OF PENHALLY BAY

*Devoted doctors, single fathers, a sheikh surgeon,
royalty, miracle babies and more... Hearts made whole
in an idyllic Cornish community*

**This Christmas meet pregnant doctor Lucy Tremayne—
will the secret surrounding her baby
tear the Tremayne family apart?**
Christmas Eve Baby by Caroline Anderson

**Enjoy some much needed winter warmth in January with
gorgeous Italian doctor Marcus Avanti**
The Italian's New-Year Marriage Wish by Sarah Morgan

**Then join Adam and Maggie in February
on a 24-hour rescue mission where romance
begins to blossom as the sun starts to set**
The Doctor's Bride by Sunrise by Josie Metcalfe

**Single dad Jack Tremayne finds a mother for his little
boy—and a bride for himself this March**
The Surgeon's Fatherhood Surprise by Jennifer Taylor

**There's a princess in Penahally! HRH Melinda Fortesque
comes to the Bay in April**
The Doctor's Royal Love-Child by Kate Hardy

Edward Tremayne finds the woman of his dreams in May
Nurse Bride, Bayside Wedding by Gill Sanderson

**Meet hunky Penhally Bay Chief Inspector Lachlan D'Ancey
and follow his search for love this June**
Single Dad Seeks a Wife by Melanie Milburne

**The temperature really hots up in July when devastatingly
handsome Dr Oliver Fawkner arrives in the Bay...**
Virgin Midwife, Playboy Doctor by Margaret McDonagh

**Curl up with Francesca and Mark in August as they
try one last time for the baby they've always longed for...**
Their Miracle Baby by Caroline Anderson

**September brings sexy Sheikh Zayed
from his desert kingdom to the beaches of Penhally**
Sheikh Surgeon Claims His Bride by Josie Metcalfe

Snuggle up with dishy Dr Tom Cornish in October
A Baby for Eve by Maggie Kingsley

**And don't miss French doctor Pierre,
who sweeps into the Bay this November**
Dr Devereux's Proposal by Margaret McDonagh

A collection to treasure for ever!

CHAPTER ONE

Early May

'Lucy.'

'Ben!' She spun around, her heart tripping and a smile she couldn't hold breaking out at the sound of his voice. 'I didn't think you'd come.'

Hoped, yes, stupidly much, even though she'd known it was an outside chance, but here he was, the answer to a maiden's prayers—well, hers, at least—and her knees had turned to mush.

'Oh, you know me, ever the sucker,' he replied with that lazy, sexy grin that unravelled her insides. 'I had my arm twisted by one of my patients, and it would have been churlish to refuse. Besides, if I remember rightly, the food's amazing.'

So, he hadn't come to see her, then, but what had she expected? Two years was a long time, and so very much had happened. Too much.

Stifling the strangely crushing disappointment, she looked away from those piercing eyes the colour of a summer sky and glanced behind her at the barbeque. 'It certainly smells fabulous. I wonder when we can get stuck in? I haven't eaten since breakfast, and that was before seven.'

'Sounds as if your day's been like mine,' he murmured, and she realised he'd moved closer. Much closer, so that she could not only hear his voice more clearly, but smell the clean, fresh scent of his skin. He never wore aftershave, but he didn't need to, not to enhance him, because the combination of soap and freshly laundered clothes, underscored by warm, healthy man, was a potent combination.

She felt herself sway a little towards him and wrenched herself back upright. 'Sorry—my heels are sinking into the grass,' she said, not untruthfully, but it gave her an excuse to shift her position and move a fraction away from him. Just far enough so she couldn't smell that intoxicating blend of citrus and musk.

'So—how are you?' he asked, his voice still soft, and even though she knew it was silly, that it didn't matter how nice he was to her, her heart opened up to his gentle enquiry.

'Oh—you know.'

His smile was wry. 'No, I don't, or I wouldn't be asking. How's general practice working out?'

She tried to inject some enthusiasm into her voice. 'It's fine. Great. I was on call last night and I had a surgery this morning, so I'm a bit tired today, but it's OK. I'm really getting into it.'

'Pity.'

She tipped her head and looked up at him curiously. 'Why?'

'My registrar's leaving—decided for some reason to throw away a promising career in favour of maternity. I don't suppose I can tempt you back to A and E?'

Oh, she was tempted. So tempted. To work alongside him again—well, opposite him, to be exact, their heads and hands synchronised, fighting together to save a patient against all odds, their eyes meeting from time to time, his crinkling with that gorgeous, knee-melting smile—but there were too many reasons why not, and one of them was insurmountable, at least for now if not for ever.

She shook her head regretfully and tried to smile. 'Sorry, Ben. Anyway, I still get to do emergency medicine, and we've got a really busy minor injuries unit.'

'What, sprains and jellyfish stings with the odd heart attack thrown in for good measure?' he teased. 'That isn't emergency medicine, Lucy.'

'We do more than that, and it's enough drama for me,' she said, ignoring the little bit of her that was yelling *liar!* at the top of its voice. 'And anyway, we've been thinking about expanding. We're already too busy in our minor injuries unit, so why not expand and make it a state-of-the-art MIU? Still walking wounded, but a bit more sophisticated than what we've got. Maybe have a dedicated space for one of the community physios instead of her just sharing the nurses' room, and ideally get our own X-ray—I don't know. And while we're at it, expand our minor surgery. We'll have to talk to the trust—see if we can convince them it's a good idea. We could take some of the heat off St Piran, especially in the summer with all the tourists.'

She was babbling, trying to ignore the bit of her that was screaming *Yes, take me back!* but he was listening as if she wasn't talking utter rubbish, and he nodded slowly.

'Sounds as if you've given it a lot of thought, and it certainly makes sense. Our A and E's running flat out, and if you've got good minor surgical facilities as well, that's all to the good. You'd need that for all the stitching of wounds in the MIU, and you could maybe take on some more complex minor surgery. I'm sure they do loads of things in the day surgery unit that don't really need a GA. If the simpler things could be done out in the community under local anaesthetic, it would shorten the waiting list, but the X-ray idea's brilliant. People often sit for hours just to be told they've got a sprain. If you could filter some of those out, maybe put casts on undisplaced fractures or reduce the odd dislocation, it could really take the heat off us. I like it. I like it a lot. I'm all for people being seen quicker and closer to home, and I'd be happy to help in any way I could.'

'I may well take you up on that in your new capacity as head honcho of A and E,' she said with a smile, her heart giddy at the idea of working with him again in any capacity at all. 'All I have to do is convince the bean counters.'

He grinned. 'I wish you luck,' he said drily. 'Whatever, I'm more than happy to advise you, if you want, and if you need any help with leaning on anyone in the primary care trust or the hospital trust for funding, give me a shout. I won't guarantee I've got any influence, but you're welcome to what little I have.' He hesitated for a moment, then added softly, 'I see your father's here. How is he, Lucy?'

Oh, lord. Her father. She shook her head slowly. 'I'm not sure, really. Sometimes he seems fine. Other times he's moody and preoccupied, as if he's still sad inside. I just get the feeling he hasn't let go. Hasn't grieved properly. I mean, it's been nearly two years, Ben, but he still doesn't talk about Mum. Not naturally, in conversation. And I want to talk about her. She was my mother, I loved her. I don't want to forget her.' She looked round, spotting her father at the barbeque, turning sausages and talking to Kate.

Kate was the backbone of the practice, his practice manager and her mother's friend. His friend first, from way back when, but nothing more than that. Sometimes she wondered if Kate would have liked it to be more, but she didn't think there was any chance of that. Not on her father's side, at least. Not unless he could move on.

'I didn't know if he'd be here. Do you think he'll object to my presence?'

'No,' she said quickly, although she wasn't sure. 'Don't be silly. It's a fundraiser, you have every right to be here. Besides, you haven't done anything wrong, and you don't have to talk to him.'

'No, I suppose not. I just didn't want to make him uncomfortable.'

She shrugged. 'It's his problem, not yours. Anyway, he's got other things to think about, and so's Kate Althorp, our practice manager. That's her, next to him—dark hair, in the pale pink top.'

'Yes, I've met her in the past. Nice woman.'

'She is. She practically runs this thing every year. Did you know her husband James was our lifeboat coxswain? She lost him, and Dad lost his father and brother, in the storm in '98.'

His brow creased into a frown. 'I didn't know that. I wasn't living here at the time, and the names didn't mean anything to me. I just remember there was a group of schoolchildren studying the rockpools and they were cut off by the tide, and some of the rescuers died.'

Lucy pointed across the harbour to the headland jutting out, crowned by the lighthouse and the church. 'It was over there.'

He was looking at the headland, his brow furrowed. 'What

on earth were the kids doing out there anyway? Weren't they supervised?'

'Oh, yes, but the teacher's watch had stopped and they didn't realise the tide was coming in until it was too late. Add in the huge sea, and you get a disaster.'

'Absolutely. I'm sorry, I didn't realise any of them were connected to you. I just remember one of them was a local doctor.'

She nodded. 'My uncle. They were trying to rescue the children from the bottom of the cliff over there, and it all went wrong. Phil—my uncle—had abseiled down the rocks and got most of them up, but the storm had got really wild by then and he was swept off the cliff by a huge wave and suffered severe head injuries. My grandfather had a heart attack and died on the clifftop just after they brought Phil's body up.'

Ben's eyes searched hers, his expression sombre. 'That must have been horrendous for you all.'

She nodded. 'Especially my father. Apart from Mum and my brothers and me, they were his entire family. He'd lost his mother a couple of years before, and his brother wasn't married. And his father was only sixty-eight.'

'And Kate's husband?'

'James? He was swept off the rocks. They sent out the inshore lifeboat to pick up the kids on the rocks at the end of the promontory, but James had a broken rib so he wasn't on the lifeboat, so he went down out onto the rocks to help a girl who was too scared to move. They threw him a line and a life-jacket, and he got it on her and tied her to the line, but the same wave that killed my uncle swept several of them out to sea and his body was never recovered.'

Ben made a sympathetic noise. 'How awful for Kate.'

'I'm sure it was, but she seems to have dealt with it pretty philosophically. As she said, the sea was going to get him one way or another. At least he died a hero.'

Ben nodded. 'It must have left a huge hole in the community.'

'Oh, yes, but my father never talks about that night. It's as if it never happened. He's always like that. Anything bad that happens, anything personal, he just shuts down.'

'I'm surprised he comes to this event.'

Lucy gave a rueful laugh. 'Oh, I don't think Kate gives him a choice. They've been friends for ever, and she pretty much organises this event every year. He just does what he's told. And anyway, it's for a good cause. The lifeboat's been part of Penhally for generations, and there's nobody who hasn't lost someone close to them or someone they knew well at some time in the past—sorry, I'm going on a bit, but I'm quite passionate about it.'

'Don't apologise. I'm all for passion. The world would be a much duller place without it.' He grinned and added, 'You can get passionate with me any time you like.'

Innocent words, said to lighten the mood, but there was something in his eyes that was nothing about lifeboats and all about passion of another sort entirely, and she felt her heart skitter. Crazy. She hadn't seen him for nearly two years, and their brief relationship had been cut off abruptly, but if it hadn't…

'Mr Carter! You came!'

He turned to the grey-haired woman with a cast on her arm and smiled and shook her other hand. 'I said I would.'

'Lots of people say that. Most of them aren't here. And you're with our lovely Dr Lucy. How are you, dear? Keeping well, I hope? I haven't seen you for a while.'

'No, you've defected and moved to Wadebridge, Mrs

Lunney,' Lucy said, grateful for the distraction. 'You look well on it—well, apart from your arm. I take it that's how you met Mr Carter.'

She smiled. 'Yes—and I'm getting married again because of it! All my neighbour and I had ever done was say hello over the fence for the past six months, but when I broke my arm Henry was just there for me, doing all sorts of little jobs without me asking, and then—well, let's just say he was very persuasive! And we're getting married next month, when I've got this cast off.'

Lucy hugged her gently. 'That's wonderful. I'm really pleased for you. Congratulations. I hope you'll both be very happy.'

'Thank you, dear. Now, you two enjoy yourselves. I'd better get back to Henry—he's a bit out of his depth here, and they'll be giving him a bit of a grilling, checking him out. You know what they're like! I'd better rescue him.'

Ben chuckled. 'You do that—and congratulations. I'm glad something good came out of your broken arm. Now,' he said softly as she walked away, 'Mrs Lunney's typical of the sort of cases we don't need to see at St. Piran. Simple, undisplaced fracture, and she had to come all that way and sit and wait for an hour and a half before she was seen and given pain relief. Crazy. You could have had her sorted out and on her way by the time she arrived at St. Piran.'

'Don't. I'm working on it, Ben, and Dad's very keen.' Partly because he didn't want anyone who didn't have to go there being sent to St Piran. Since her mother…

He lifted his head and cocked an eyebrow towards the food. 'Looks like we're on,' he said, and she fell into step beside him, dragging her mind back to the present.

'Thank goodness for that. I'm going to fade away in a minute! That piece of toast was much too long ago.'

They joined the queue, many of them known to her, either as patients or old friends of her family, and several of the villagers recognised Ben from their trips to the A and E department, so as the queue moved steadily towards the food they were kept busy chatting.

She picked up two plates and handed one to Ben, and then they were there in front of the massive oildrum barbeque, and her heart sank. She'd hoped her father might have moved on to do something else, but he was still there beside Kate, turning sausages and piling up steaks and burgers, and he lifted his head and paused, a sausage speared on a long fork hovering in mid-air.

Ben met his eyes and inclined his head the merest fraction in acknowledgement.

'Dr Tremayne, Mrs Althorp,' he said, and Lucy felt her pulse shift up a notch. It was inevitable that they'd end up running into each other, but now, watching as they eyed each other in silence like stags at bay, she conceded that maybe Ben had been right about not being here.

For an awful, breathless moment she thought her father was going to make a scene, but then he handed the fork to Kate, muttered something to her and walked off.

'He's just remembered something he had to do,' Kate said apologetically, but she couldn't look them in the eye and Ben shook his head and turned to Lucy with a strained smile and handed her the plate.

'I'm sorry, I appear to have lost my appetite. Enjoy the rest of the party.'

And he turned on his heel and strode away through the

crowd, heading for the gate that led out of the car park. Lucy
turned back to Kate, her eyes wide with distress.

'Why is Dad like this? Why can't he just get over it?' she
said helplessly.

'I don't know. I'm sorry, Lucy. Can I get you anything?'

She looked across the crowded car park. Ben had turned
the corner, gone through the gate into Harbour Road, but she
could still catch him…

'No. Sorry, got to go!' she said, turning back for a moment
to dump the plates back on the pile. Ignoring the damage to
her high heels, she sprinted across the car park and through
the gate into the road and followed him. He was just revers-
ing his sleek BMW convertible out of a space, and she ran
over to the car and wrenched open the passenger door.

'Ben, wait!'

'What for?' he asked, his eyes bleak. 'I shouldn't have
come, Lucy, it was stupid of me. I'm out of here.'

'Me, too,' she pointed out, sliding in beside him and
shutting the door. 'After all, we have to eat, and we're all
dressed up with nowhere to go. It seems a bit of a waste.'

'I don't know. I don't think I'll be very good company.'

'I'll risk it,' she said, holding her breath. 'We could always
get fish and chips.'

For a moment he just sat there, the engine idling, and then
he gave a ragged laugh and cut the engine. 'Go on, then. Go
and buy them. Here—take this. I'll wait here.' He handed her
a twenty-pound note, and she ran over the road to the chippy.
It was deserted, because everyone was at the barbeque, so
she was served quickly. She put the change into the Penhally
Bay Independent Lifeboat Association collecting tin on the
counter and ran back to Ben.

He was staring sightlessly out to sea, his eyes fixed on the horizon, and she slid into the seat beside him and gave him a smile. 'I gave your change to the PBILA,' she told him, and he gave a crooked smile.

'How appropriate. Right, where to?'

'Somewhere quiet?'

He grinned. 'I know just the place.' Starting the engine again, he nosed out into the crowd, drove slowly down Harbour Road and then, as they left the crowds behind, he dropped the clutch and shot up out of the village along the coast road with a glorious, throaty roar. The sun was low over the sea, but it was behind them and once past the caravan park he hit the accelerator, the car hugging the curves and dips of the road as if it were on rails.

She gathered her long, tumbled curls in one hand and turned to him, raising her voice to be heard over the roar of the engine and the rush of air. 'So where are we going?' she yelled.

'There's a viewpoint along here, and we can catch the sunset. It's my favourite place,' he said, his eyes fixed on the road, and she nodded.

'Good.'

And at least no one from Penhally Bay would be there. They were all safely at the barbeque. She settled back in the seat, and waited for the sick feeling in her stomach to settle.

'That was fabulous.'

He crumpled up the paper and wiped his hands on it. 'It was—and probably no more unhealthy than a barbeque, even if it was the most expensive fish and chips I've ever had,' he added pointedly.

'I'm sorry,' she said feeling a flicker of guilt, but he just grinned.

'Don't be. Fancy a stroll?'

'In these shoes?' She laughed.

'You'd be all right in bare feet on the sand.'

'But I have to get there, and I won't get down those steps in these heels.'

'I'll carry you,' he said.

'Don't be ridiculous,' she told him, but she took her shoes off anyway and started to pick her way over the stones to the edge of the car park, wincing and yelping under her breath.

'Idiot,' he said mildly, and, scooping her into his arms and trying not to think too much about the feel of her warm, firm body against his chest, he carried her down the steps and set her on her feet on the sand. 'There,' he said, and he heeled off his shoes, stripped off his socks and rolled his trouser legs up to the knee. 'Last one in the water's a sissy,' he said, and sprinted towards the sea.

She couldn't resist it. He'd known she wouldn't be able to, and he let her catch him, grabbing her hand at the last moment and running with her into the surf.

Just ankle deep, and so early in the year that was enough, but it brought colour to her cheeks and laughter to her brown eyes, and then the laughter faded and she lifted her hand and rested it against his cheek.

'Ben, I'm so sorry about my father...'

He turned his head and kissed her palm gently. 'Don't be. It's my fault. I suspected he'd be there and I should have stayed away.'

'But he was so rude to you.'

'I can cope with it. It's my own fault, but I hoped you'd

be there, and you were, so let's forget about your father and just enjoy being together. Come on, let's walk for a bit.'

It was like something out of a film set. They were strolling beside the water, their hands still linked, and it was wonderful—romantic, peaceful, with the sun's last rays gilding the rippling surface of the sea. But he was unsettled, churned up inside by his encounter with Nick Tremayne and going over it all again and again, as if it would change the past.

Stupid. It was over—finished. He put it out of his mind and turned to Lucy. The sun was about to slip below the horizon, a pale gold orb hovering just above the surface of the sea, the sky shot through with pink and gold, and he put his hands on her shoulders and turned her, easing her against him so her back was warm against his chest, and he held her there motionless as together they watched it flare, then sink into the sea and disappear.

'I never get tired of watching it set,' she said softly. 'I can see it from my sitting-room window at this time of year, and I love it. I can quite see why people worship the sun.'

She turned slowly and lifted her head, her eyes gazing up at him. They were beautiful, the softest brown, warm and generous. Windows on her soul. Such a cliché, but so, so true, and for the first time that day Ben felt she was really letting him in. He felt his pulse pick up, felt the slow, heavy beat of his heart against his ribs, the first stirrings of need.

'Have I told you how lovely you look today?' he said a little unevenly.

She let her breath out in a little rush that could have been a laugh but might just have been a sigh. 'No. No, you haven't.'

'Remiss of me. You look fabulous.' He ran his eyes over her, over the soft gauzy dress that was cut on the cross and clung gently to those slender curves. It was sea-blue, not one colour but many, flowing into each other, and with the surf lapping at her ankles, she could have risen from the water.

'You look like a siren,' he said gruffly, and then without stopping to think, he leant forward, just a fraction, and low-ered his mouth to hover over hers. 'Luring me onto the rocks,' he added, his words a sigh.

And then he touched his lips to hers.

For a moment, she just stood there, her eyes staring up into his, and then her lids fluttered down and she shut out every-thing except the feel of his lips and the sound of the sea and the warmth of his hands on her shoulders, urging her closer.

She didn't need urging. She was ready for this—had been ready for it for ever—and with a tiny cry, muffled by his lips, she leant into him and slipped her arms around his waist, resting her palms against the strong, broad columns of muscle that bracketed his spine.

He shifted, just a fraction, but it brought their bodies into intimate alignment, and heat flared in her everywhere they touched. She felt the hot, urgent sweep of his tongue against her lips and she parted them for him, welcoming him in, her own tongue reaching out to his in greeting.

He groaned, his fingers tunnelling through her hair, and steadying her head with his broad, strong hands, he plundered her mouth, his body rocking against hers, taut and urgent and, oh, so welcome. She heard herself whimper, felt him harden, felt his chest heave in response, and she thought, We can't do this. Not here. But she couldn't stop, couldn't drag herself out of his arms, couldn't walk away…

'Lucy.'

He'd lifted his head, resting his forehead against hers, his breath sawing in and out rapidly. 'What the hell are we doing?' he rasped softly.

What we should have done years ago, she thought. She lifted her hand and cradled his jaw. 'Your place or mine?' she murmured, knowing it was stupid, knowing it was the last thing she ought to be doing but unable to stop herself.

He lifted his head and stared down into her eyes, his own smouldering with a heat so intense she thought she'd burn up.

Then the ghost of a smile flickered over his taut features. 'Mine,' he said gruffly. 'It's not in Penhally. And it's closer. Come on.'

And freeing her, he slid his hand down her arm, threaded his fingers through hers and led her back to the steps, pausing only to hand her his shoes before scooping her up and carrying her up the steps and across the stones to his car.

'Ouch,' he muttered, limping, and she laughed breathlessly.

'That'll teach you to behave like a caveman,' she teased, and he dumped her over the door into her seat, vaulted past her and slid down behind the wheel.

'I'll give you caveman,' he growled, and she felt a delicious shiver of anticipation.

'Want your shoes?'

'No. The only thing I want is you,' he said tautly, gunning the engine and shooting backwards out of the space, then hitting the coast road in a spray of granite chips while she grappled for her seat belt and wondered if it had been quite wise to wake this sleeping tiger...

'Lucy?'

She opened her eyes and stared up at him, reaching up a hand to rub it lightly over the stubble on his jaw. That siren's smile hovered on her lips, rosy and swollen from his kisses, and he wanted to kiss her all over again. 'Well, if it isn't my very own caveman,' she said softly.

He laughed, then bent his head and touched his lips to hers, tasting her smile. 'Good morning,' he murmured, his mouth still on hers, and he felt her lips curve again.

'Absolutely,' she replied, and opened her mouth to his, drawing him in, her arms sliding round him and cradling him closer. He felt the heat flare between them, felt her pelvis rock, felt the soft, moist heat of her against his thigh as she parted her legs to the urging of his knee.

Hell. He hadn't been going to do this again. He'd been going to talk to her, to tell her all the reasons why this was such a lousy idea, but her body was hot and naked against his, her soft, welcoming flesh too much for him to resist. He'd wanted her for years, ever since they'd worked together, and if it hadn't been for her mother's death…

Damn.

He shifted, pulling away, but she followed him, her hands holding him to her, rolling after him and taking over, her body hot and sweet and so, so lovely, and as she lowered herself and took him inside her, he lost rational thought.

He groaned her name, arching up as she rocked against him, taking him deeper, and then, grasping her hips, he drove into her again and again, feeling her passion build, feeling the tension spiral in her until her breathing grew ragged and she sobbed his name. He felt her body contract around him, felt the incredible power of her climax, and followed her head-long over the edge.

It was her phone that woke them, ringing from somewhere downstairs in the depths of her handbag.

'I'll let it ring,' she said, but then it rang again, and again, and finally she got up. ran downstairs naked and answered it.

He followed her slowly, pulling on his dressing-gown and going into the kitchen to put on the kettle, the shirt he'd worn the previous day flung over his shoulder.

'Dad, I'm fine. No, I'm not at home,' she was saying as he threaded her arms one at a time into the shirt. 'I'm twenty-nine years old, for heaven's sake! I don't need your permission to leave my house on my day off!'

She rolled her eyes at Ben, and he smiled faintly and turned back to the kettle, listening by default to her side of the conversation as he made them tea.

'Yes, I'm sorry, too. Yes, I think you do. Yes, I'll tell him if I speak to him. OK. I'll see you on Tuesday, after the bank holiday.'

He heard her cut the connection, heard the soft sound of her bare feet on the floor and turned with a smile. 'You looked a little underdressed,' he said, glad now that he'd covered her because she looked sexier in his shirt than he could have imagined in his wildest fantasies.

'Thanks.' She threw him a fleeting smile and pulled the shirt closed, buttoning it and running her hands round the neck and lifting her hair out in a soft, gleaming tumble of curls that made him want to gather them in his hand and tug her gently back to his arms. Or bed. Whatever. Closer, anyway.

He turned back, poured the tea and handed her a mug instead. 'What did your father want?'

'To apologise for being rude to you yesterday. He said he owed you an apology, too. He asked me to tell you if I saw you.'

Ben grunted. Nick Tremayne probably did owe him an apology after yesterday, and if he hadn't just spent the night with the man's daughter Ben might have been less forgiving. As it was, he just felt sick at heart and deeply sorry for everything that had happened, even though it hadn't been his fault.

He wondered if Lucy really believed that he wasn't to blame, or if somewhere deep inside there was a bit of her that wasn't quite sure. He must have been crazy to bring her back here last night and complicate things like this...

'Ben?'

He glanced up at her, his face sombre, and she felt her heart sink.

'This isn't going to work, is it?'

'Us?' He shook his head and sighed softly. 'No.'

She felt tears sting her eyes and blinked them away. She wasn't going to cry. She wasn't. 'Too much baggage.'

He didn't reply. There was nothing more to add.

So that she didn't have to go home in the same dress everyone had seen her in the day before, he lent her a pair of denim cut-offs that were loose on her waist and snug on her hips, and the shirt she was already wearing, and drove her home. He pulled up outside her front door. Gathering her things together, she paused, her hand on the car door.

'Thank you for last night, it was wonderful,' she said, and, leaning over, she kissed him goodbye.

It seemed horribly, unbearably final.

CHAPTER TWO

Mid-November

'RIGHT, Lucy and Dragan, don't forget I've booked you both off this afternoon for the MIU meeting with the St Piran consultant. He's coming about two-thirty,' Kate said.

'Pointless,' Nick said flatly. 'I don't know why you've booked him in with Lucy. Can't you reschedule it for when I'm around? She won't be in a position to implement the changes and we've got more than enough to think about at the moment. We won't need all the extra hassle while we've got a locum in. I think we should forget it for now.'

'No,' Marco interjected. 'The community needs more than we can offer, Nick, and we do need to do this as soon as we can. We've talked it over endlessly.'

'So why Lucy? Why not us? It's our practice.'

'Because she's the most appropriate person,' Kate pointed out calmly. 'Apart from the fact that you've shown no interest in being involved in this up to now, emergency medicine is her area of responsibility in the practice, and this was all her idea. It's only a feasibility study, Nick,' she went on, 'planning for the future. Someone's got to do it, so why not her? Besides,' she added before Lucy could interrupt and point out that she was still, actually, in the room, if they'd all finished talking about her, 'they've worked together before, so it makes sense.'

They had? When? Or more importantly…

Nick's brow pleated into a scowl. 'Who is it?' he asked, yet again before Lucy could speak.

'Oh—didn't I mention that?' Kate said guilelessly. 'It's Ben Carter.'

'Ben?' Lucy said, her heart lurching against her ribs. Oh, no. Not Ben! Not when she still hadn't told him…

Her father's frown deepened. 'Carter!' he growled. 'Why the hell is *he* coming?'

'Because he, like Lucy, is the most appropriate person for the job—and he volunteered.'

Really? Why on earth would he do that, seeing that the last time she had spoken to him it had been to agree that they shouldn't see each other again because of the situation between him and her father?

Nick was emphatic. 'No. Not Carter. I don't want him in my practice.'

'Our practice,' Marco pointed out mildly. 'And anyway, it's irrelevant what you or I or anybody else want. If we're going to do this, we need an expert, and he's the best.'

'Rubbish, the man's incompetent.'

'Dad, no! You cannot go around saying things like that about him.'

'Why not, if it's the truth?'

'Because it isn't! The inquiry exonerated him absolutely.'

'It was a whitewash. Utter whitewash, and if you weren't so hoodwinked by the man you'd realise it.'

'Nick, that's not fair,' Kate said gently. 'He's very well regarded.'

He stood up and banged his mug down on the draining-board. 'Think what you like, he's the last person we need here,' he said stubbornly. 'It doesn't matter what any of you say, you'll never convince me otherwise. Ben Carter's bad news, and I don't want anything to do with him.'

He spat Ben's name as if it were poison, and Lucy's heart sank. Was he ever going to be able to see this clearly? Because if not…

'Nick, you're getting this totally out of proportion,' Kate said firmly. 'Anyway, you don't have to have anything to do with him. You're busy with your antenatal stuff, Marco's concentrating on the paeds, this is all Lucy and Dragan. Mostly Lucy. And if they're all happy about it, I really don't see why it's such an issue. It's not as if he's going to be having any involvement in the running of the unit.'

Nick opened his mouth to reply, but Marco cut him off.

'She's right. Move on, Nick. Let it go.'

He shut his mouth, opened it again, and then turned abruptly and stalked towards the door. 'Fine. Don't any of you mind me, I'm just the senior partner,' he snapped, and slammed the door shut behind him.

Lucy winced, Marco shrugged, Dragan shook his head and frowned and Kate smiled briskly at everyone and headed for the kettle. 'Right. That's that settled. Coffee, anyone?'

Lucy couldn't believe it was Ben.

Of all the people to be coming, why did it have to be him?

Although she had to see him some time, and preferably soon. Unless she just wasn't going to…

No. That wasn't an option. She just wanted time to think it through, to work out the words, to find a way of introducing the subject.

Ridiculous. She'd had months to talk to him, months to think up the words. She was just a coward—a coward with a patient who was staring at her a little oddly, waiting.

'Right, Mrs Jones, I'm sure you'll be all right. I'm confident that as I first thought it's just a little bit of fluid on your lungs from your heart problem, so I'm juggling your pills a little and we'll see if you improve. Here's your new prescription, but in the meantime the injection I've just given you should start to shift it soon, and the extra frusemide should do the trick in the long term.' She clipped her bag shut with a little snap, and picked it up. 'If I don't hear anything from you, I'll come back and see you next week to make sure it's cleared up, but if you're at all worried, you call me, OK? No being stoic.'

Edith Jones nodded. Recently widowed, she was struggling to cope with her new independence, and Lucy worried about her. Her heart condition had been fine until her husband's sudden and traumatic decline, and since then she'd been neglecting herself. Not any more, though. Lucy simply wouldn't let her. Edith was still a little breathless, but even in the short time since Lucy had given her the diuretic injection, she'd noticed an improvement.

'I'll be fine, Doctor,' Edith said with a smile. 'Thank you so much for coming.'

'My pleasure. You stay there, I'll let myself out.'

'No, that's all right, I'll see you to the door. I have to get up to go to the toilet anyway. That's one of the problems with your medicine!'

Good. More evidence of the drugs working, but just to be on the safe side, Lucy warned, 'Don't forget to keep drinking. I don't want you thinking you can keep the fluid off your lungs by dehydrating yourself. That's not how it works. Cut down on your salt intake, and have lots of water and fruit juice, and not too much of that mega-strong tea you like to drink, or you'll be getting problems with your waterworks to make life even more interesting! And don't forget—if you aren't entirely convinced it's working, ring me.'

'I will, Doctor. Thank you.'

She waved goodbye, got into her car and drove the short distance back to the surgery. It was ten past two, and Ben would be arriving in twenty minutes. Just time for a bite of lunch and a little hyperventilation before she had to see him again...

He was early.

He hadn't meant to be, but the morning had gone badly and he hadn't stopped for lunch in case the roads were busy, then they'd been clear and he'd found himself at the practice at five past two. So he was sitting in his car and killing time, staring out over the harbour and wondering whether he should go in and what kind of reception he would get from Nick Tremayne.

Hopefully better than the reception he'd got in May when he'd come to the barbeque here. Still, Nick had agreed to their meeting, so presumably Lucy had finally talked him round. Not that he expected miracles. A chilly silence would be more like it, but even that might be better than outright hostility.

A vessel caught his eye, a little fishing smack coming into the harbour, running in on the waves. The sea beyond the harbour mouth was wild and stormy today, the water the colour

of gunmetal. It looked cold and uninviting, and he was glad
he didn't make his living from it.

He turned his head and studied the cars in the car park,
wondering which one of them was Lucy's. The silver Volvo?
No. That was most likely to be Nick's. The little Nissan?
Possibly. Not the sleek black Maserati that crouched menac-
ingly in the corner of the car park, he'd stake his life on it.
That, he'd hazard a guess, was Marco Avanti's.

He was just psyching himself up to get out of the car and
go inside when a VW turned into the car park and drove into
one of the spaces marked 'Doctor'.

Lucy. His pulse picked up, and he took a slow, steadying
breath to calm himself. After all, the last time he'd seen her
had been in early May, and they'd both made it clear it wasn't
going anywhere. He was sure they could be adult about this—
even if it had taken weeks to get her out of his mind again.

Longer still to get her out of his dreams, but he'd done it,
finally, by working double shifts and staying up half the night
trawling the internet in the name of research. And he was over
her. He was.

So why was his heart racing and his body thrumming?
Crazy. He shouldn't be here. He should have let someone else
do it—one of the other A and E guys…

She was getting out of the car, opening the door, and in
the rear-view mirror he could see her legs emerging, and then
her…body?

He was on his feet and moving towards her before he had
time to realise he'd moved, before he'd thought what he was
going to say, before he'd done anything but react. And then,
having got there, all he could do was stare.

'Ah, Mr Carter, welcome!'

He realised Kate Althorp was beside them, talking to him, and over the roaring in his ears he tried to make sense of it. She was holding out her hand, and he sucked in a lungful of air, pulled himself together and shook it, the firm, no-nonsense grip curiously grounding. 'Ben, please—and it's good to see you again, Mrs Althorp. Thank you for setting this up.'

'Call me Kate—and it's my pleasure. Lucy, I've put tea and biscuits out in my office for you, so you won't be disturbed. Dragan Lovak's had to go out on a call—he'll be joining you later. But since we're here now, why don't we have a quick guided tour before the clinics start, and then I'll leave you both to it?'

And he was led inside, Lucy bringing up the rear, her image imprinted on his retinas for life. He followed the practice manager through the entrance to Reception, smiling blankly at the ladies behind the counter, nodding at the patients in the waiting room, vaguely registering the children playing in the corner with the brightly coloured toys. He saw the stairs straight ahead, easy-rising, and the consulting rooms to the right, on each side of the short corridor that led to the lift.

'It's a big lift,' Kate was saying as the doors opened and they stepped in. 'Designed for buggies and wheelchairs and so on, but not big enough for stretchers, although we don't have any call for them really. If people collapse and have to go to hospital in an ambulance, they've probably been in to see one of the doctors, and as most of the consulting rooms are downstairs anyway, that's more than likely where they'll be. If not, the paramedics usually manage to get them down in the lift without difficulty. The trouble is the building wasn't designed to be a surgery, so it's been adapted to make the best use of what we have.'

'How long has the practice been here?'

'Two years. After Phil died there wasn't a practice here in Penhally Bay until two years ago. A neighbouring practice closed and they lost the last of the local doctors, and Marco Avanti and Nick set up the practice here where it is now to fill the gap.'

The lift doors opened again and he found himself at the end of a corridor the same as the one downstairs, with rooms to left and right. 'We've got the nurses' room and a treatment room up here, and our MIU, such as it is. I'll let Lucy show you that, she'll know more about it than me.'

'What about a waiting area?' he asked, forcing himself to concentrate on something other than Lucy. She was going through a door marked 'Private', closing it firmly behind her. Damn.

'We have a couple of chairs out here but we don't tend to use them except in the summer when it's busier,' Kate was saying. 'Usually they call the patients up one at a time from downstairs. Our staffroom and shower and loo are up here, too, as well as another public toilet and the stores, and this is my office.'

She opened the door and ushered him in. 'Have a seat,' she said. 'Lucy won't be a moment. I'll put the kettle on.'

He didn't sit. He crossed the room, standing by the window, looking out. It was a pleasant room, and from the window he could see across the boatyard to the lifeboat station and beyond it the sea.

He didn't notice, though, not really. Didn't take it in, couldn't have described the colour of the walls or the furniture, because there was only one thing he'd really seen, only one thing he'd been aware of since Lucy had got out of her car.

The door opened and she came in, and with a smile to them both Kate excused herself and went out, closing the door softly behind her, leaving them to it.

Lucy met his eyes, but only with a huge effort, and he could see the emotions racing through their wary, soft brown depths. God only knows what his own expression was, but he held her gaze for a long moment before she coloured and looked away.

'Um—can I make you some tea?' she offered, and he gave a short, disbelieving cough of laughter.

'Don't you think there's something we should talk about first?' he suggested, and she hesitated, her hand on the kettle, catching her lip between those neat, even teeth and nibbling it unconsciously.

'I intend to,' she began, and he laughed and propped his hips on the edge of the desk, his hands each side gripping the thick, solid wood as if his life depended on it.

'When, exactly? Assuming, as I am, perhaps a little rashly, that unless that's a beachball you've got up your jumper it has something to do with me?'

She put the kettle down with a little thump and turned towards him, her eyes flashing fire. 'Rashly? *Rashly?* Is that what you think of me? That I'd sleep with you and then go and fall into bed with another man?'

He shrugged, ignoring the crazy, irrational flicker of hope that it was, indeed, his child. 'I don't know. I would hope not, but I don't know anything about your private life. Not any more,' he added with a tinge of regret.

'Well, you should know enough about me to know that isn't the way I do things.'

'So how do you do things, Lucy?' he asked, trying to stop

the anger from creeping into his voice. 'Like your father? You don't like it, so you just pretend it hasn't happened?'

'And what was I supposed to do?' she asked, her eyes flashing sparks again. 'We weren't seeing each other. We'd agreed.'

'But this, surely, changes things? Or should have. Unless you just weren't going to tell me? It must have made it simpler for you.'

She turned away again, but not before he saw her eyes fill, and guilt gnawed at him. 'Simpler?' she said. 'That's not how I'd describe it.'

'So why not tell me, then?' he said, his voice softening. 'Why, in all these months, didn't you tell me that I'm going to be a father?'

'I was going to,' she said, her voice little more than a whisper. 'But after everything—I didn't know how to. It's just all so difficult…'

'But it *is* mine.'

She nodded, her hair falling over her face and obscuring it from him. 'Yes. Yes, it's yours.'

His heart soared, and for a ridiculous moment he felt like punching the air, but then he pulled himself together. Plenty of time for that later, once he'd got all the facts. Down to the nitty-gritty, he thought, and asked the question that came to the top of the heap.

'Does your father know it's mine?'

She shook her head, and he winced. 'So—when's it due?'

'The end of January.'

'So you're—'

'Thirty weeks. And two days.'

He nodded. That made sense, but there was another question that needed answering. 'You told me you were on the Pill.'

She bent her head. 'I was, but because it was only to regulate my periods I probably hadn't been as punctual all the time as I should have been. I used to take it in the morning, but I didn't remember till the Tuesday, by then it was too late.' Because she'd been crying since the moment she'd closed her front door behind her on Sunday morning and retreated into the sanctuary of her little home, wearing his shirt day and night until she'd had to take it off to shower and dress to come to work after the bank holiday, and then she'd found the pills...

'So why not take the morning-after pill just to be safe?'

Why not, indeed? She shook her head. 'I didn't have any, and by the time I was able to get them from the pharmacy it would have been too late. And anyway, I thought I was safe,' she told him, and wondered, as she'd wondered over and over again, if there'd been a little bit of her that had secretly wanted to have his baby. And when her periods had continued for the next two months, she'd put it out of her mind.

Not for long, though. Eventually it had dawned on her that things were different, that the lighter-than-usual periods had been due to the hormones, and she'd kept it a secret as long as she could. Eventually, though, the changes to her body had become obvious, and her father had been shocked and then bossily supportive.

And he hadn't asked about the father, not once she'd told him that he was out of her life for good and she didn't want to think about him any more. Not that she had wanted Ben out of her life, but he was, to her sorrow and regret, and she didn't want to think about him any more. She'd been sick of crying herself to sleep, missing him endlessly, wishing he could be with her and share this amazing and fantastic thing that was happening to her body.

Her stomach rumbled, and she gave the biscuits a disinterested glance. OK, she could eat them, but she really, really wanted something healthy, and if Dragan was held up…

'Have you had lunch?' she said suddenly.

'*Lunch?*' he said, his tone disbelieving. 'No. I got held up in Resus. There wasn't time.'

'Fancy coming back to my house and having something to eat? Dragan can ring when he's on his way back and we can meet him here. Only I'm starving, and I'm trying to eat properly, and biscuits and cakes and rubbish like that just won't cut the mustard.'

'Sounds good,' he said, not in the least bit hungry but desperate to be away from there and somewhere private while he assimilated this stunning bit of news.

She opened the door, grabbed her coat out of the staffroom as they passed it and led him down the stairs. 'Kate, we're going to get some lunch. Can you get Dragan to ring me when he's back?'

'Sure,' Kate said, and if Lucy hadn't thought she was being paranoid, she would have sworn Kate gave her and Ben a curiously speculative look.

No. She couldn't have guessed. It had been months since she'd seen them together.

Six months, one week and two days, to be exact. And Kate, before she'd become practice manager, had been a midwife.

Damn.

They walked to her flat, along Harbour Road and up Bridge Street, the road that ran alongside the river and up out of the old town towards St Piran, the road he'd come in on. It was over a gift shop, in a steep little terrace typical of Cornish coastal towns and villages, and he wondered how she'd manage when she'd had the baby.

Not here, was the answer, especially when she led him through a door into a narrow little hallway and up the precipitous stairs to her flat. 'Make yourself at home, I'll find some food,' she said, a little breathless after her climb, and left him in the small living room. If he got close to the window he could see the sea, but apart from that it had no real charm. It was homely, though, and comfortable, and he wandered round it, picking up things and putting them down, measuring her life.

A book on pregnancy, a mother-and-baby magazine, a book of names, lying in a neat pile on the end of an old leather trunk in front of the sofa. More books in a bookcase, a cosy fleece blanket draped over the arm of the sofa, some flowers in a vase lending a little cheer.

He could see her through the kitchen door, pottering about and making sandwiches, and he went and propped himself in the doorway and watched her.

'I'd offer to help, but the room's too small for three of us,' he murmured, and she gave him a slightly nervous smile.

Why nervous? he wondered, and then realised that of course she was nervous. She had no idea what his attitude would be, whether he'd be pleased or angry, if he'd want to be involved in his child's life—any of it.

When he'd worked it out himself, he'd tell her. The only thing he did know, absolutely with total certainty, was that if, as she had said, this baby was his, he was going to be a part of its life for ever.

And that was non-negotiable.

* * *

What on earth was she supposed to say to him?

She had no idea, and didn't know how it could be so hard. When they'd worked together, he'd been so easy to talk to, such a good friend, and they'd never had any tension between them. Well, that was a lie, but not this sort of tension.

The other sort, yes—the sort that had got her in this mess.

No. Not a mess. Her baby wasn't a mess, and she wasn't ever going to think of it as one.

She put the sandwiches on plates, put the plates on a tray with their two cups of tea and carried them through to her little living room. 'Sit down, Ben, you're cluttering the place up,' she said softly, and with a rueful little huff of laughter he sat, angled slightly towards her so he could study her.

Which he did, with that disconcertingly piercing gaze, the entire time she was eating her sandwich.

'We could get married,' he said out of the blue, and she choked on a crumb and started to cough. He took the plate and rubbed her back, but she flapped him away, standing up and going into the kitchen to get a glass of water.

And when she turned he was right behind her, so close that she brushed against him, her bump making firm and intimate contact with his body. For a moment he froze, and then his eyes dropped and he lifted a hand and then glanced back up at her, as if he was asking her permission.

She swallowed slowly and nodded, and he laid his hand oh, so tenderly over the taut curve that was his child. Something fierce and primitive flickered in his eyes, and then he closed them, and as the baby shifted and stretched she watched a muscle jump in his jaw.

His hand moved, the softest caress, and he opened his eyes, lifted his head and met her eyes.

'I felt it move,' he said, and there was wonder in his voice, and joy, and pride.

And for the first time she felt the tension ease and some of the dread fade away.

'It'll be all right, Lucy. Don't worry. I'll look after you.'

'We aren't getting married, Ben.'

'Don't close your mind to it,' he said softly.

'It's too soon.'

'Of course it is—but it's one of our options.'

Ours?

She would have moved away from him, but he had her pinned up against the sink and in the narrow kitchen there was nowhere to go. So she turned her back to him, but it didn't help because he simply moved up closer, sliding his arms around her, resting both hands on her tummy and drawing her gently back into his warm embrace. 'Don't be scared.'

'I'm not scared,' she lied. 'I just don't like you turning up out of the blue and telling me what to do.'

'Out of the blue? I hardly abandoned you, Lucy. The last conversation we had, you told me it wasn't going to work. Too much baggage.'

'And you agreed.'

'So I did,' he said thoughtfully. 'But that was then, and this is now, and things are different. The baggage certainly is. I can't let you face your father alone.'

'And you really think you being there, telling him you're the baby's father, will help?'

He sighed and moved away at last, giving her room to

breathe, to re-establish her personal space and gather her composure around her like a security blanket.

'Come on,' he said. 'You haven't finished your sandwich. Come and sit down and put your feet up and tell me what you were planning.'

She laughed wryly. 'I didn't have any plans,' she confessed, feeling suddenly lost again. 'I was just winging it, getting through a day at a time. And Dad hasn't really asked very much about the baby's father. Just how could I have been so silly and that I'd have his support. He wants me to move back in with him, but I don't want to.'

'Lucy, you can't stay here,' he said, his voice appalled, and she felt her mouth tighten.

'Why not? Don't come in here and start insulting my home, Ben.'

'I'm not insulting your home, sweetheart, but look at it. It's tiny, and it's up a steep hill and a narrow flight of stairs, with no parking outside—where do you keep your car? The surgery? That'll be handy in the pouring rain when you've got a screaming baby and all your shopping.'

She bit her lip, knowing he was right and yet not wanting to admit it. Of course the flat wasn't suitable for a baby, and she'd been meaning to find somewhere else, but anything rented was usually in holiday lets in the summer, and she couldn't afford those rates, not unless she went back to work, and buying somewhere in the village on a part-time salary probably wasn't an option either.

'I don't suppose he's any nearer to accepting that I wasn't to blame for your mother's death?' he suggested, and Lucy shook her head.

'I don't think so. He wasn't very pleased this morning when Kate announced that it was you coming.'

A frown pleated his brow. 'Really? But it was decided weeks ago. Kate said everyone was fine with it. I assumed he must know.'

She met his eyes, and realisation dawned. 'She's worked it out,' she said slowly. 'She knows you're the father. Well, at least, she knows I don't have a life outside Penhally, because she can see the surgery car park from her house up behind it, and she'll know my car's always there unless I'm out on a call or visiting friends, and she can see my window here—that's her house over there,' she said, pointing out to him the pretty little cottage tucked against the hillside above the surgery. 'So there's nothing I can do without her knowing, and if I had a man, believe me, Penhally would be talking about it. And the last man I was seen with was you, and of course she knows we'd worked together, that we were friends.'

'I don't know how you can stay in this place,' he said gruffly, and sighed. 'You reckon she knows?'

'I think so. She gave us a look as we left the surgery.'

'A look?'

'Yeah—one of those knowing ones.'

He grinned a little crookedly. 'Ah. Right. And do you think she'll tell your father?'

Lucy felt a little bubble of hysterical laughter rising in her chest. 'I wish. Maybe that way he'd calm down before I had to talk to him about it.'

'You really think it'll be that bad?'

She stared at him blankly. 'You don't have any idea, do you? Because you haven't seen him since Mum died, apart from the lifeboat barbeque. Ben, he—' She broke off, not knowing quite how to put it, but he did it for her, his voice soft and sad.

'Hates me? I know. I've already worked that out. And I can see why.'

'But it wasn't your fault!' she said, searching his face and finding regret and maybe a little doubt. 'Ben, it wasn't. The inquiry exonerated you absolutely. Mum died because she didn't tell anyone how sick she was until it was too late. I wasn't there, Dad was too busy setting up the practice with Marco, and she downplayed it just too long.'

'Lucy, she died because when she arrived in the A and E department she didn't check herself in straight away, so nobody flagged her up as urgent, nobody kept an eye on her, nobody realised she was there until they found her collapsed in the corner. There'd been a massive RTA, there were ambulances streaming in, we were on the verge of meltdown—I don't have to explain it to you. You know the kind of mayhem I'm talking about, you've seen it all too often. I was trapped in Resus, the walking wounded were way down the list. Too far. And the other people waiting just thought she was asleep, instead of which she'd all but OD'd on painkillers and by the time we got to her it was too late.'

'They said her appendix had ruptured. She must have been in so much pain. I knew she'd been feeling rough but I had no idea how rough. It must have been agony.'

'Yes. Hence the painkillers. She'd obviously had a hell of a cocktail. We found codeine and paracetamol and ibuprofen and aspirin in her bag. The codeine must have knocked her out, but it was the aspirin that killed her. By the time she arrived at the hospital, she was too woozy to talk to anyone. The CCTV footage shows her stumbling to a chair in the corner and sitting down, and because she didn't check in or tell anyone how bad she felt, she was overlooked until it was too late. You know how aspirin works—it's an anticoagulant, like warfarin, and it stops the platelets clumping to arrest a bleed in the normal way. And with the rupture in her abdomen, she just bled out before we could get to it. If your father hadn't phoned her mobile, she wouldn't have been found until she was dead. It was only because the phone kept ringing and she was ignoring it that the alarm was raised. And we did everything we could at that point, but it just wasn't enough, and everything we touched was breaking down and starting another bleed. And I can tell you how sorry I am for ever, but it won't bring her back.'

She shook her head and squeezed her eyes shut to close out the images, but they wouldn't be banished, and she knew her father had seen it because they'd called him immediately to ask if he knew why she might be there, and he'd arrived while they had been in Resus, fighting for her life, and had insisted on going in. It must have been hideous for him, but it didn't change the facts. 'It wasn't your fault,' she told Ben yet again.

'I was in charge. I know I wasn't a consultant then, but I was the most senior person in the department that day, and so the responsibility rested with me.'

'You're not God.'

'No. So I needed to be more careful, because I don't just know everything, but things are different now that I'm a consultant and actually have some say. It couldn't happen now. All patients are intercepted on their way into the department by the triage nurse, people waiting are checked at regular intervals, and I insist on being constantly alerted to what's happening in my department. I can't let it happen again.'

'Ben, you didn't let it happen. You weren't negligent.'

'Maybe not. But I can see where your father's coming from, and I wouldn't want a man I thought was responsible for the death of my wife, no matter how indirectly, being the father of my grandchild.'

'Well, he's going to have to get over it,' she said firmly, 'because you are the father—unless we just aren't going to tell him?'

'That's not an option, Lucy,' he said, shaking his head. 'This baby may not have been planned, but it's mine, and I fully intend to be involved in its life. And I can't do that in secret. I can't, and I won't, so, come what may, your father has to know.'

But how? She had no idea, but at least now Ben was in the picture. One down, one to go, she thought.

But then he went on, 'I know you'll say it's too soon, and you're probably right, but I intend to look after you and my baby for the rest of your lives, so get used to the idea.'

She sat up straighter, absently massaging the bump. 'Out of a misplaced sense of duty? No, Ben. It has to be more than that. I agree, I can't stay here, but I'm not moving in with you any more than I'm moving in with my father. I don't want to be someone's duty. I'm sick of duty. I want love for my baby. And for me. Nothing else.'

'It will be love.'

'It will. From me, for a start. But we're part of a package, the baby and I, and we're both equally important, and I'm not going to do anything hasty. You and I haven't seen each other for months, and that was a one-off. You weren't even ready to carry on seeing me because things were too difficult. Well, if they were difficult before, they're much worse now, and I'm not going to do anything until I'm sure the time is right.'

'Right with who?'

'With me—with you—with my father.'

His jaw tensed, the muscle working, and he turned away. 'OK. So—you need accommodation. Somewhere we can have some privacy so I can share my baby with you without causing any of you unnecessary grief—is that what you're suggesting? That we duck around, grabbing a few minutes together every now and then when your father and the rest of Penhally Bay aren't looking? No. It's my baby, Lucy, and I'm damned if I'm going to be ashamed of it. Your father can just learn to deal with it, and the rest of this flaming community can just learn to mind their own business.'

She stared at him, then with a choked laugh she turned away, picked up the tray and stood.

'If you imagine for a moment that's going to happen, Ben Carter, you're in cloud cuckoo land,' she said, and, taking the tray through to the kitchen, she dumped it down and brushed off her hands. 'We'd better get back to the surgery.'

'I thought Dragan was going to phone you.'

'So did I, but he's obviously been held up. There's a lot we can achieve without him, so let's get on with it.' And without waiting for him to reply, she picked up her coat, slid her arms into it and headed for the door.

CHAPTER THREE

THERE was no sign of Nick, thank goodness. Ben had been in suspense, waiting for him to appear, but he noticed the silver Volvo was gone, so maybe he could relax for now. Not for ever. He knew that, but if they were going to have a confrontation, he'd rather it wasn't in a crowded surgery in front of half of Penhally Bay's insatiably curious residents.

There was no sign of Dragan Lovak either, and Ben wondered if Kate had sent him off on a wild-goose chase or told him that they'd gone for lunch and to take his time. If Lucy was right, that wasn't beyond the realms of possibility.

Whatever, Lovak wasn't there to keep them on the straight and narrow, and he had to force his attention back to the Penhally Bay surgery's MIU and away from the smooth, firm protrusion that was his child.

'Have you had a scan?' he asked abruptly, and Lucy stopped talking and turned and looked at him in frustration.

'You haven't heard a word I've said, have you?'

He opened his mouth to deny it, then shook his head. 'Sorry. I'm finding it a bit hard to focus.'

She sighed and reached out a hand, but then thought better of it and withdrew it. 'Look—are you busy tonight? I've got a surgery from five to six-thirty, but I'm not doing anything later. If you're free, perhaps we could talk then? Deal with some of your questions?'

He nodded, a little shocked at how eager he was to have that conversation—a conversation about a child that until a very short while ago he hadn't even known existed. 'Of course.'

'And for now,' she said, her voice gently mocking, 'do you think you could keep your eyes on my face and concentrate on what I'm saying about our minor injuries unit?'

'Sure.'

He nodded, swallowed and tried to smile, but it was a feeble effort and he just wanted to fast-forward to the evening and get the hell out of there.

'Come and see what we have,' she said, and led him into the room in question. It was about twice the size of a consulting room, on the upper floor, and not ideal. He forced himself to concentrate.

'It needs to be bigger and it could do with being on the ground floor,' he told her without preamble.

'We know that. We're looking at funding for expansion.'

He nodded.

'In the meantime, this is what we have and what we do. There's a room next door where we do minor surgery, but it really is minor and very non-invasive—skin lesions, ingrowing toenails and the like. It's more of a treatment room, it's not a proper theatre, although of course we use sterile techniques, but I don't think we can realistically create a dedicated theatre environment either in there or anywhere else in a general practice setting. It simply isn't called for, but it's adequate for what we do surgery-wise. And this room is where we do all our minor injury stuff that we handle at present.'

'Such as?'

'Oh, all sorts. If I tell you the areas that we can currently cover and where I feel the holes are in our provision, maybe you can give me some advice on what we'd need both short and long term to improve that?'

'Sure.'

'Good. Right. Well, in the summer, we get tourists, of course, who as well as coming for medical treatment come to the MIU with things like stings, sprains, cuts and fractures. You'd be surprised how many people travel without a first-aid kit.'

He chuckled. 'No, I wouldn't. We get them all the time.'

'Of course you do. I forgot,' she said, smiling at him and dragging his mind away from medicine and onto something entirely more interesting.

'Then all year round but particularly in the warmer months we have surfers with all their associated injuries—scrapes on rocks, collisions with their own surfboards and with others, the odd weaver fish and all the other touristy things, and we get anyone who needs more than the basic first aid the life-guards give on the beach, but our baseline local population is farmers and fishermen and their families, so we have a lot of work-related injuries. I've lost count of the number of tetanus shots I've given in the last year. We do a lot of nee-dlework, obviously—cuts and tears, many of them dirty, so we have a certain amount of debriding to do. Some have to come to you because they're too extensive and need plastics or specialist hand surgery, for example. And we have frac-tures, lots of simple undisplaced fractures and dislocations that with X-ray we could deal with here if we had plaster fa-cilities. They'd still need the care of the orthopaedic team for anything more complex, of course, but there are so many little things we could sort here locally.'

He nodded. 'I agree. The medical emergencies are still going to have to come through us, but from the point of view of straightforward physical injury you could take a lot off us.'

He looked around the room, noting the two couches, the chairs and trolleys and screens, the bench along the side with pretty much the same equipment you would find in a practice nurse's room or one of the cubicles in his A and E department, but for the most part that was all that would be necessary.

'What about resuscitation equipment?'

'Standard GP stuff for an isolated rural practice. We've got a defib and oxygen and a nebuliser, of course, and 12-lead ECG and heart monitor…'

She rattled off a list of things they had and things they wanted, leaving nothing out that he felt would be in any way useful or necessary, and he was impressed.

'You've done your homework,' he said softly, and she stopped and stared at him, giving an exasperated sigh.

'Did you really think we'd get you over here to talk this through if we hadn't? I want this to work, Ben. We need it. We're too far from St Piran. Some of the injuries we see—if we had better facilities so we could just treat them here, at least initially… That journey must be horrendous if you've got a fracture. It's not so much the distance as the roads—so narrow, so twisty, and lots of them are rough. The main road's better, but reaching it—well, it doesn't bear thinking about, not with something like a spinal injury or a nasty compound fracture. We have to fly some of our surfers out just for that reason, because they'd have to come to you, but for the others—well, it's just crazy that we can't do it. There's certainly the demand.'

'I'm sure. You know, if you weren't about to be taking maternity leave, it would make sense for you to come and spend some time in the department. Catch up on your X-ray, diagnostic and plastering skills.'

'I could do that anyway—well, not the X-ray, not until the baby's born, but the rest. I'm going to be coming back to work—I can't afford to stop— And don't say it!' she ordered, cutting him off before he could do more than open his mouth.

So he shut it again, shrugged his shoulders and smiled wryly. 'So where are you going to site the X-ray machine?' he asked. 'Bearing in mind that the room needs screening on all six sides?'

'Out on the end of the sea wall?' she suggested, eyes twinkling, and he chuckled.

'Nice one. Not very practical, though. Do you have a spare room?'

She laughed wryly. 'Not so as you'd notice. In an ideal world, as Kate says, it would all be on the ground floor, but down in the old town like this it's difficult. The sides of the cove are so steep, so all the houses are small and on top of one another. The only way around it would be to build it up out of the town, and that's not where it's needed.'

'Unless you sited it up near the church, halfway between the old town and the beach. Handier for the tourists and all the people staying in the caravan park, and no harder for the people you serve who don't live right in the centre and have to come by car anyway.'

'Except that when we tried to sound them out we couldn't get planning permission and, anyway, any site up there which they'd allow development on would have such stunning sea views it would be worth shedloads and we couldn't afford it, so it's academic. This is what we have, Ben. And there's room to extend at the back—behind the stairwell there's an area of garden which isn't used for anything except sneaking out in breaks and having a quiet sit down out of earshot of the locals. And we're so busy that that isn't really an option in the summer, and in the winter—well, frankly it's not very appealing, so really it's dead space.'

'Can I see?'

'Sure.'

She led him downstairs, snagging her coat from the staff-room on the way, and they went out the front and round the side, between the boatyard and chandlery and the end of the surgery building. 'Here,' she said, pointing to an area that was behind the waiting room and stairs.

He nodded approval, running his eyes over it and measuring it by guesswork. 'It's ideal. It's big enough to make a proper treatment area for suspected fractures and house the X-ray facilities, and you could put further accommodation on top—a plaster room, for instance, and somewhere for people to rest under observation. And you'd still have the existing room upstairs which you could use for other injuries, cuts and such like, jellyfish stings, weaver fish—you name it. Or you could relocate one of the consulting rooms currently down-stairs upstairs to that area and use more of the downstairs space for those things, so you've got all your injuries together. And weren't you talking about physio? That probably needs to be downstairs…'

She started to laugh, and he broke off and scrubbed a hand through his hair ruefully. 'OK, so it's not big enough for all that, and it's robbing Peter to pay Paul, but I don't see what else you can do. If you want to do this properly, you'll have 'to compromise. And you'll have to sell it to the people who'll be compromised.'

'Except my father doesn't want me involved, because I'm going to be on maternity leave. He thinks he should be doing it, but it's not his area of expertise, and I really wanted to oversee it, to make sure it works,' she said softly, the smile fading from her eyes and leaving a deep sadness in its place.

And Ben felt guilty—hugely, massively guilty—because all he'd done by taking Lucy back to his house and making love to her had been to cause her even more grief to add to the emotional minefield that was her life. 'It'll work, Lucy. I'm sure it will—and by the time you come back to work it'll be ready for you to commission.'

'I'm sure you're right,' she said, but she didn't sound it.

She shivered, and he frowned and turned up her coat collar, tugging it closer round her. 'You're cold. Come on, let's go back inside and jot some of this down, do a few doodles...'

'I've done some. I'll show you. And we can have tea.'

The universal panacea. He smiled. 'That would be good. Come on.'

She led him back inside, shivering again and realising that she'd let herself get chilled. It wasn't cold—in fact, it was incredibly mild overall—but the wind was blustery today and cut right through her.

'Kate, is it OK to use your room still?' she asked, leaning over the counter and smiling a greeting at the receptionist, Sue.

Kate put her hand over the receiver and nodded. 'Sure. Go on up. Oh, and Dragan's on his way in—he's bringing Melinda. She's been bitten by a dog. That's why he's been held up. He asked if you could see her. I think she needs suturing.'

'Oh. Right. Can't Dad see her, or Marco?'

'No. Your father's gone over to the house to meet the agent, and Marco's got a clinic, so if you wouldn't mind fitting her in?'

'No, sure. Send them up. I'll use the treatment room upstairs,' she said, and felt the tension draining out of her at the news that her father had gone out and wasn't about to pop out of the woodwork at any moment and cause a scene.

She headed for the stairs, still thinking about her father and not really conscious of the extra effort it took to mount them now that she was pregnant, but evidently Ben noticed because as she arrived at the door of the staffroom he asked, 'How long are you planning to work?'

His voice had a firm edge to it and she looked up at him questioningly.

'Today? Till six-thirty.'

'In your pregnancy.'

'Oh.' So he was doing the proprietorial father bit, was he? 'Till I have the baby,' she said defiantly, and then, before he could argue, qualified it with, 'Well, as long as I can, really. I'll cut out house calls soon, especially if the weather gets bad, and I've already stopped doing night calls. That's one of the advantages of being a pregnant woman in a practice of three single men—they're so busy fussing over me and taking work off me I have to fight them for every last patient!'

His mouth twitched, and he gave a soft laugh. 'And I bet you do.'

'Absolutely. I don't need to be pandered to,' she told him firmly. 'I'm pregnant, Ben, not sick.' She filled the kettle and switched it on, made them two mugs of tea and picked them up. 'Can you get the doors, please?' she said, and he dutifully led her through into Kate's room and shut the door behind them.

She plonked the mugs down on Kate's desk, took the plans of the surgery from the drawer in the filing cabinet and smoothed them out, then laid her tracing-paper alterations over the top. 'Right, this is what I'd thought could be done,' she said, and launched into her explanation.

He couldn't fault it.

She knew just what she wanted and, apart from a very few suggestions, there was nothing she'd planned he wouldn't have been more than happy with in their situation.

He told her so, pointed out the few changes he'd make, and they did some little scribbles on the tracing paper, then she sat back and rubbed her tummy and winced.

'Braxton Hicks?' he guessed, and she nodded.

'Yes. It's beginning to drive me mad. Every time I sit still for any length of time I get them, over and over again. I swear I don't need any more practise contractions. My uterus is going to be so toned up by the time I give birth it's ridiculous.'

'I suppose you're sure of your dates?' he said, and then immediately regretted it because she glared at him as if he'd lost his mind.

'As there was only the one occasion,' she snapped, 'it would be hard to miscalculate.'

'Three, if I remember correctly,' he murmured.

'Three?'

'Occasions,' he said, and she coloured and turned away with a little sound of frustration.

'That's irrelevant.'

'Not to me,' he said. Her colour deepened and she stood up and walked over to the window, rubbing her back. He got up and followed her, standing by her side and drawing her against him, putting the heel of his hand into the small of her back and massaging it firmly while he held her steady against his chest.

Silly girl. She needed him, and he wasn't going to let her get away with this independent nonsense a minute longer.

For a moment she stood stiffly, then with a ragged little sigh she leant into him, dropped her head forward and gave herself up to the comfort of his touch. It just felt so good to have him hold her, and she'd missed that so much, having someone to hug her and hold her. Her mother had always hugged her, and her father used to, but her mother was gone and her father had shut down and now there was no one.

Except Ben, and his hand was moving slowly, rhythmically round on her back, easing out the kinks in her muscles and soothing the tension. And she would have stood there for ever, but she heard footsteps outside and a tap on the door, and she stepped away from Ben just as Dragan put his head round the door and smiled.

'Hi. Sorry I'm late. I've got Melinda here—Kate said you'd look at her?'

'Sure. Hi, Melinda,' she said, greeting the young vet who was fast becoming a treasured part of their community. 'I gather you've been bitten?'

'Yes—stupid,' she said, her slight Italian accent at odds with the gorgeous golden blonde of her hair. She tossed it back over her shoulder out of the way and it slid forward again, obviously irritating her. 'It was my own fault. The dog was injured—we found her on the road near the pub. We'd been for lunch to the Smugglers' and we were on the way down when we saw her. She was in pain, she didn't know me—it was just one of those things.'

'Is she OK?'

'She is now,' Dragan said drily. 'We had to follow her, of course, and catch her, and then take her to the surgery and put her in a cage to rest. I had to drag Melinda here.'

'I could have cleaned it up myself—'

'It's bleeding much too fast. You need serious attention, the right antibiotics—'

'You think I don't have antibiotics suitable for dog bites?' she said mildly, but she held out her left arm to Lucy, her right hand holding down a blood-soaked swab on the inside of her forearm. 'He's right. It is bleeding heavily. I think she's nicked one of the vessels.'

'Let's go into the treatment room and have a look. Oh, by the way, sorry, Dragan Lovak, Melinda Fortesque, Ben Carter,' she said economically, getting the introductions over and ushering her into the treatment room where they did their minor surgery. 'Let's have a look at it,' she suggested. Easing off the pad of gauze, she winced at the bloody mess and pressed the pad quickly back in place over the briskly bleeding vein.

'Ouch.' Ben leant over her shoulder. 'May I take a closer look in a moment?'

'Of course,' Melinda said.

'Nasty bite. We need to clean it thoroughly,' Lucy said as Ben joined her at the basin and started scrubbing.

'That vein needs suturing,' he murmured. 'Are you happy to do that or do you want me to have a go? Assuming it's something we can tackle here?'

She shrugged uncertainly. 'Well, I can have a go,' she said.

'Have you got any fine suture material?'

'I believe so. I don't suppose, since you're here…? We might as well take advantage of the head honcho—you're bound to be better than me, your skills are more up to date than mine.'

He chuckled. 'I doubt if that's true, but if you're happy for me to do it to save sending her to St Piran?'

'Of course I am. It's not my arm, of course, but I'm sure Melinda doesn't want to go to St Piran either.'

'No, I don't,' she said promptly from behind them. 'I have to get back to the dog, and I don't care which of you does it so long as one of you does.'

'Right, let's take a look at it before we make any rash promises,' Ben said. Snapping on gloves, he settled down on a stool next to the couch and studied the wound, blotting it frequently with a gauze swab to keep the field clear of blood. 'Looks sore.'

'It is sore. Some local wouldn't hurt before you go poking it.'

He chuckled and met her eyes with a smile that made Lucy feel instantly, absurdly jealous. Dragan, too, unless she was much mistaken, and she wondered what the situation was between them. Something, otherwise he would have done this himself, but what?

Lovers? Friends? Two strangers in a strange land? Dragan was Croatian, and he'd been living in England since his teens. He didn't talk about his past, but there were shadows in his eyes, and as for Melinda, although Lucy knew little about her past there was an air of quiet dignity about her that hinted at breeding. Yet even so, she was open and friendly and down-to-earth, and anyone more lacking in airs and graces she could hardly imagine.

She looked up at Dragan to say something, and found him watching her, his brooding eyes thoughtful. Then his eyes dropped to Ben, and back to her, and she thought, Good grief, is it so obvious? Do I have a sign on my bump that says, *Child of Ben Carter* on it?

Or was she just reading something that didn't exist into his expression?

'Lucy, can we put a cuff on the arm to cut off this blood supply? And can I have some saline to irrigate this, please?' Ben asked, and she stopped worrying about Dragan and what he was thinking and concentrated on doing her job—or rather helping Ben do his, which she had to admit he was doing beautifully.

He numbed the area and sutured the vessel so neatly Lucy could only watch in awe, then he cleaned the wound thoroughly and released the cuff to check his suturing had worked. 'Good,' he murmured, and trimmed away the little flaps of skin that had lost their blood supply and drew the edges of the wound together with Steristrips. The whole thing had only taken him a few minutes.

'There,' he said, flexing his shoulders and nodding in satisfaction. 'That should sort you out. I can't suture the skin because of the high risk of infection, but the tape should hold it together well enough. Keep it dry, though—and I think you should have a broad-spectrum antibiotic. They've discovered bugs in dog bites that they didn't know infected humans, so I like to provide a broader cover than a simple penicillin type. Lucy, could I have a sterile non-adherent dressing, please?'

'Sure.' She handed him the pack, found the tape and helped him dress the wound.

'OK,' he said, sitting back with a smile. 'Hopefully it'll heal fast, but I'm afraid you might end up with a scar.'

Melinda shrugged and smiled. 'It won't be the first—occupational hazard. Thank you, Ben. Now I can get back to my patient.'

'How's your tetanus?' Lucy asked, and she laughed.

'Well and truly up to date. I got bitten last year. You'd think I'd learn but apparently not.'

Ben chuckled. 'Right, Lucy had better give you your prescription—and you'll need painkillers. Something with codeine, probably, and a non-steroidal. And look out for reddening, fever, swelling, shivering and anything else unusual in the next week. OK?'

'OK. And thank you so much. Right, now I *must* get back to this dog.'

'You should get someone else to do it,' Dragan said, frowning, but she brushed his suggestion aside.

'No. She's frightened, that's all. She's only young, and she was hurt. She's not vicious. I'll get a nurse to help me, we'll be fine.'

He muttered something unintelligible and foreign under his breath. 'I should be here, we're meant to be having a meeting, but you haven't got your car,' he said to Melinda, and Lucy shook her head and handed over the prescription.

'Don't worry, Dragan, you give her a lift back. We've talked it all through and, anyway, I've got a surgery starting in a few minutes. We'll catch up tomorrow and I'll fill you in, and we'll schedule another meeting in a week or two.'

He nodded and, shaking Ben's hand and thanking him, he ushered Melinda out, leaving them alone.

She was about to offer him more tea when Ben glanced at

his watch. 'Right, I suppose I ought to shoot off. I'll pick you up tonight—from here? Six-thirty?'

She shook her head. The last thing she wanted was him picking her up from the surgery when her father was likely to be lurking around. 'I'll meet you somewhere at seven. Your house?'

He nodded. 'Fine. Do you still know the way?'

Know it? She'd almost worn out the road, toing and froing, desperate to see him and yet unable to bring herself to ring the bell and tell him she'd made a mistake about them not being together. And then she'd found out she was pregnant, and she had been wearing out the road for another reason, trying to screw up the courage to tell him that.

'Yes, I know the way,' she said. 'I'll see you there. And make it eight. That'll give me time to get home and eat something.'

'No. I'll feed you.'

'Seven-thirty, then,' she agreed, because for some perverse reason she wanted to go home after her surgery, shower and change into something—well, something else. Something pretty. Something that didn't make her feel like a heffalump.

She walked him back down to Reception, sent him on his way and went into her consulting room, watching him through the window as he got into his BMW and drove away.

It was nearly five. The lights were on in the village, twinkling all around the harbour and giving it a cosy feel, and she could imagine how it must be to enter the harbour mouth and see the lights of home ahead of you.

Safe. Reassuring.

And unaccountably she thought of Ben. Her eyes tracked to his car, following the lights out of the village, along

Harbour Road, up Bridge Street and past her front door, out of sight.

Two and a half hours, she told herself, and felt a little shiver of something she hadn't felt for a very long time.

'Kate?'

The knock on the door came again, and Kate opened it to find Nick standing there, hands rammed deep into his pockets, a brooding look on his face. She frowned in concern.

'Nick—hi. What can I do for you?'

'Oh, I was just— I've been clearing the last of the things out of the house. It seems so odd—end of an era. The agent's expecting a good turn-out at the auction, but I've told him to lower the reserve. He was putting a high one on with a view to marketing it in the spring if it doesn't go, but I told him no. I just want it gone.'

'And you're feeling lost.'

'Not at all. Has to be done,' he said briskly.

But Kate knew him better than he knew himself, she sometimes thought, and she knew just how hard he'd be finding this. His mother's family home, the place he'd been born and raised in, the house his father had been living in at his death. The sale had been a long time coming, but he'd got there in the end. Maybe he'd always imagined retiring there with Annabel in the future, but of course that wouldn't happen now, and the pointlessness of owning it had gradually come home to him.

Poor Nick. He'd lost so much. 'I'm sure the sale will be a great success,' she said just as briskly. 'Some Londoner who wants to divide their time—someone with a family who'll come down and spend quality time together, bring it to life again. Just what it needs, and you'll be able to take a nice long holiday on the proceeds. Got time for coffee?'

'I suppose so. Thanks—yes, coffee would be lovely.'

He followed her through to the kitchen and propped himself up against the island unit, watching her while she made their drinks. 'Where's Jem?' he asked.

'In bed—Nick, it's nearly ten.'

'Is it?' He sounded startled, and checked his watch disbelievingly. 'So it is. I'm sorry—want me to go?'

'No, you're fine,' she said. 'Let's go and sit down.'

She handed him his coffee and led him through to the sitting room. He sat beside her on the sofa, propping his feet on the box that served as a coffee-table and resting his head back with a sigh. 'I'm bushed,' he confessed.

'Of course you are. Clearing the house was always going to be hard. You should have asked for help.'

'No.'

Nothing else, just the one word. Then he sat up straighter and looked down into his coffee. 'Do you know where Lucy is?'

'At home in bed, I imagine, if she's got any sense.'

'Her car's not at the surgery. It's always there.'

'Perhaps she's out meeting friends. Maybe they've gone out for a meal or something. She sometimes goes out with Chloe and Lauren.'

'But if she's not—if she's in trouble…'

'Nick, she's fine.'

'I'm going to ring her.'

'No. Let me do it. If you really insist, let me do it. She won't bite my head off.'

She put her coffee down, got up and went into the kitchen.

Quite unnecessarily, because it was a cordless phone, but she wanted Nick out of earshot. 'Lucy, your father's worried,' she said when Lucy answered. 'He noticed your car wasn't there. I said you'd probably gone out for a meal with friends.'

There was a heartbeat of silence, then Lucy said, 'Um— yes, I have.'

'I thought so,' Kate said, reading between the lines. 'You enjoy yourself—and don't worry about him.'

There was another tiny hesitation, then Lucy said softly, 'Kate, keep him off my case.'

'Sure. I'll see you tomorrow.'

'Thanks.'

Kate hung up and went back into the sitting room.

'Well?'

'She's out for dinner with friends—I told you she would be.'

'She never goes out without telling me. I wonder if she's with the father?' Very likely, Kate thought, knowing that Lauren was out with Martin, Alison's little one wasn't well, and Chloe was on call, but kept it firmly to herself as he went on, 'If I knew who it was who'd left her to give birth and bring up her child alone, I'd hang him out to dry. How she got herself in this mess—'

'Oh, Nick, leave the girl alone. She's a mature, independent professional woman. She's perfectly capable of fighting her own battles.'

'Is she?'

'Yes, of course she is.'

'So how did she end up like this? And how's she going to manage? For God's sake, I was only eighteen when Annabel got pregnant. We managed. And it was twins! And then we had Edward far too soon afterwards, but still we coped. We

stuck together, we made a family—for all the good it's done,'
he added despairingly. 'Lucy's pregnant and alone, Jack's got
some bee in his bonnet about cosmetic surgery, he's been running around London with one tarty little it-girl after another
and won't speak to me, and Edward can't hack it in the army.
So why the hell did we bother? Sometimes I think it's a good
thing Annabel isn't around to see it.'

'Oh, Nick.' Kate sat back with a sigh. 'You really are
down in the dumps, aren't you? You and Annabel did a fantastic job bringing up your children. You gave them every
chance you could, they've all ended up qualified doctors and
they're all doing well. You should be proud of them. What
more could you want?'

'To know my daughter's marrying the father of her child?
A man worthy of her? To know my sons aren't going off the
rails—although if either of them would talk to me it would
be an improvement—'

'And when did you last try and talk to them?'

He went silent.

'I thought so. Give them space, Nick, contact them—send
them a text, tell them you're thinking of them. Tell them
about the house. Anything. Tell them you love them. Just
don't nag.'

He snorted, and she took his mug out of his hand and stood
up. 'Come on, it's time you went home. I need to go to bed
and so do you. You look exhausted. It'll all feel better in the
morning.'

'Will it?'

His face was bleak, and she realised he was thinking about
Annabel, about going home alone to an empty house. She
knew all about that. Oh, she had Jeremiah, and she adored

every hair on his precious little head, but her bed was still cold and lonely at night.

'Goodnight, Nick,' she said firmly, and shut the door on him.

CHAPTER FOUR

'Was that Kate?'

Lucy nodded and sighed, pushing her hair back off her face and running her fingers through it absently. 'I'm sorry. Apparently my father was worried. He must have seen that my car wasn't there and my lights were off. I expect he panicked. He's such a worrywart.'

She looked troubled, and Ben just wanted to hug her, but he didn't want to push it. Instead he tried the gentle voice of reason. 'I can understand his concern. He's lost a lot of people in his family. That would make him overprotective even if you weren't pregnant and alone. And if he didn't know you were going out.'

'Oh, I know, but I just feel stifled—as if I have to log a flight plan every time I go to the supermarket! That's why I won't live with him, although in some ways it might be easier because I could just let him fuss me and give up fighting, but he'd drive me mad in a week.'

That made him smile. He could imagine her frustration but, like her father, he didn't want her living alone. Not now. Not with the baby so close. He settled back on the sofa and looked across at her curled up at the other end, her slender legs tucked up beneath her, the blatant fecundity of that smooth, round curve bringing out his paternal instinct in spades. 'So—if you aren't staying in your flat, and you don't want to live with your father, and you won't let me bully you into living with me—where do you want to live?' he asked, trying hard to keep his voice casual. 'If you could choose anywhere, regardless of anything.'

Her expression was wistful. 'Really? Total fantasy? My grandparents' house,' she said, surprising him. 'It was my grandmother's family home for ages—the farmhouse, originally, although her brother died without a family and so she inherited it, and they sold off the farm and kept the house. It's gorgeous. It's a bit rundown now. I went over there with Dad the other day and it was looking so tired. That's where he was this afternoon, clearing it out after the tenant left. He was elderly and he's left it in a bit of a state, and it needs so much work if it's going to be let again that Dad's finally decided to get rid of it. It's being auctioned this week.'

'Really?' His attention sat up and took notice of that, because his own house, dull and safe and just a stop-gap until he found somewhere with a bit more character, had been sold. That was why he was asking her, because now would be a perfect time to tailor his choice of new house to something that would fit her dreams. He'd lost the house he had been after, but he'd already accepted an excellent cash offer on his own house. The contracts had been exchanged, it was just a matter of settling the moving date—and that might just put him in a very good position...

'I feel ridiculously sad about it going out of the family,' Lucy was saying, her voice echoing her feelings, 'and I think he does, too, but there's no point in him keeping it, and I can't afford it, and there's no way my two bachelor brothers would bother with it. It's not a huge house, only four proper bedrooms and a bit of an attic, and it needs serious updating, but it's got fabulous sea views, lovely garden—I adore it. So that's my fantasy. Silly really.'

He felt a ripple of excitement. 'Not at all. It sounds lovely. What's it called?'

'Tregorran House.'

He made a mental note, but it wasn't necessary. 'Have you got internet access?' Lucy was asking, and he nodded.

'Yes—why?'

'It's on the agent's website,' she told him, and within minutes he had it all. The details, the date of the auction, the guide price, the viewing arrangements and the location.

'It looks pretty.'

'Oh, it's very tired and rundown,' she pointed out. 'Not that it matters. I won't go again. The only good thing is the council has rejected any suggestion of developing the site, so I know it'll stay as a home for some lucky family. Just not mine.'

She turned away from the computer, and he clicked the little heart that made it a favourite place so he could find it again when he next logged on, and shut it down.

She was back on the sofa, looking a little uncomfortable and very tired. He went over to her, hunkered down next to her and took her feet in his hands, lifting them onto his thigh and rubbing them gently.

'Oh, that's lovely,' she sighed, and he shifted so he was kneeling and her feet were in his lap, and she closed her eyes and sighed again. She was looking so tired. Lovely, but so, so tired. Worn down by the worry of all this, of not knowing what to do about her father and her accommodation, and he wanted so much to help her, to ease that burden, and yet he'd caused it.

Ben's hands slowed and stopped, and he realised she was asleep. Very carefully and gently he lifted her legs up and swung them round onto the sofa, and she made a little noise and snuggled down. He took off his sweater and tucked it around her, then sat down by her feet and watched her while she slept. The baby was moving, her bump shifting and wriggling, and he watched it, fascinated, for what seemed like hours.

And then suddenly her eyes flew open, screwed up then she wailed and struggled to her feet.

'What is it?' he asked, panicking, and she grabbed her calf and muttered something pithy under her breath about idiots.

'Cramp!' she yelled when he asked her again. 'Can't you see I've got a cramp?'

'So sit down and give me your leg,' he ordered, stifling the urge to laugh at his reaction. He pushed her carefully back onto the sofa and took the leg out of her hands, bending her foot up, stretching out the muscle and massaging it firmly until it softened under his hands and she groaned with relief.

'Sorry,' she said meekly, but he didn't care about what she'd said, what she'd called him, because he'd been holding her leg up in the air and trying really, really hard not to notice that under the pretty, clingy little jersey dress she'd put on for the evening she was wearing the most outrageous lacy knickers.

He dropped her leg as if it was red hot and moved away. 'OK now?'

She nodded and hauled her skirt down, but it was too late for that, the damage was done. She yawned, sighed and made to get up, and he sat down next to her and reached out a hand, resting it gently on her knee.

'Stay.'

'Stay, as in good dog?'

He smiled and shook his head. 'Stay with me. You're tired, you shouldn't be driving when you're tired.'

'And sleeping with you is any more sensible?'

'Why not? It's not as if I'm going to get you pregnant.'

She laughed and stood up, moving away from him. 'Why on earth do you want me to stay, Ben? I'm fat, I'm waddling…'

He thought of the knickers. 'No. You're pregnant. You're not fat, and you're not waddling.'

'Humph.'

'Well, not much,' he said, trying to suppress a smile. 'And you're still the most beautiful woman I've ever seen.'

'You're such a liar.'

'No. You are—beautiful and funny and warm and intelligent and sexy as hell.'

'Sexy?' she said, as if he was mad.

The knickers popped into his head again. 'Yes. Sexy,' he said firmly. 'Desirable. Gorgeous.'

'I'm pregnant,' she said sceptically.

'Yes. And still sexy as hell.'

She rolled her eyes. 'Oh, I get it. You're one of those men with a thing about pregnant women…'

'Only when they're carrying my child.'

Her jaw dropped fractionally, and she shut it and turned her head slightly. He could almost hear the cogs turning.

'Lucy?'

She looked back, soft colour touching her cheeks. 'Ben, I— This is a really lousy idea.'

'Why? I'm not walking away. I fully intend to be there for you and the baby for ever. Why not start now? You don't even have to sleep with me. I've got a spare room.'

She laughed a little oddly. 'Bit late for that.'

He wanted to go to her, scoop her into his arms and carry her up to bed, but he forced himself to be still, to wait there for her to make the first move.

But she didn't. She stood there, her lip caught between her teeth, her eyes wary. 'Ben, what if—'

'What if—what?' And then he realised. She was afraid that when she took her clothes off he'd change his mind, find her unattractive. Crazy, silly woman. Not a chance. 'Please?' he said softly. 'I just want to hold you.'

And that must have been enough, because her eyes filled with tears and she nodded, and then she was in his arms and he was carrying her up the stairs, laughing and protesting that he'd put his back out if he wasn't careful. Once he'd put her down on the edge of the bed he sat beside her and stroked the hair back from her face.

'Do you want a T-shirt to sleep in?' he asked, knowing she'd be shy, and she nodded. He pulled a long one out of his drawer and handed it to her. 'There's a new toothbrush and some toothpaste and clean towels and stuff in the bathroom. You go first,' he said, and shooed her in that direction, then turned back the quilt, stripped off his clothes, went into the *en suite* shower room and cleaned his teeth, then ran downstairs and brought up the tealight holder from the dining table and lit the candles.

He turned out the light, contemplated stripping off his jersey boxers and thought better of it, then got into bed.

He heard the loo flush, the water running, the door open,

the light click off, and then she was there, hovering in the doorway, her face troubled in the candlelight. He held his arm out to her in invitation.

'Come and have a cuddle,' he said gently, and after another moment's hesitation she slipped into bed beside him.

'Oh! It's chilly,' she murmured, and he tucked her up against him so that the firm bulge of her tummy was snuggled against his abdomen and her legs were tangled with his, and gradually, as all he did was hold her, he felt the tension ease out of her and her body relaxed against him.

God, it felt good to have her in his arms. He could feel the baby kicking, and he wondered how on earth she could rest while it fidgeted about like that. Then he got to wondering whether it was a boy or a girl, and if he cared, and he decided he didn't, just so long as everything was all right.

And then he heard a soft snore, and with a wry chuckle he shifted slightly so her head was on his shoulder and not his arm. Tucking the quilt around her shoulders to keep out the draughts, he closed his eyes and lay there and thought about the future.

He didn't know what it would bring, but one thing he was sure of—he and Lucy would be together, with their child, come hell or high water.

It was still dark when she woke up.

Dark, and warm, and deep inside her pillow she could hear a heart beating. Hers?

She shifted her legs, and found they wouldn't move because they were tangled in—legs? Hard, muscular legs, hairy legs, long and lean and definitively masculine.

And her arm was draped across a lean, firm abdomen, her hand resting on a deep chest that rose and fell steadily.

Ben. Safe and solid and apparently not in the least interested in her if last night was anything to go by.

She lifted her head a fraction and tried to ease away, but the arm around her back tightened and eased her back again. 'Don't go.'

'I need the loo,' she said, and he sighed and released her.

The candles had gone out, and she couldn't see where she was going. She heard the bed creak, felt the mattress shift, and the bedside light came on. 'OK?'

'Fine. Thanks.'

'Want a drink?'

'Oh. Water?'

'Want tea? It's nearly six. I have to get up soon.'

'Tea would be great,' she said, and then hurried to the bathroom as the baby shifted against her bladder and reminded her of why she'd woken up. And she sat there on the loo, looking down at this huge blimp that was her body now, and thought, He didn't want me. He just held me all night, and he didn't want me—not once he'd seen me like a beached whale in a T-shirt.

And she felt a stupid, stupid urge to cry. After all, she hadn't wanted to sleep with him, hadn't wanted him to initiate anything, and she'd been really tired.

Now, though, she was perversely disappointed, and she flushed the loo and had a quick wash and cleaned her teeth and wondered if she had time to get dressed again before he got back to the bedroom with the tea.

The answer was no. He was in bed, a mug on each bedside table, and he had his hands locked behind his head so she could see the broad expanse of his chest, lightly scattered with soft, dark hair, his arms powerful and strong. She knew they were strong. They'd lifted her last night as if she weighed nothing, and she remembered that the last time he'd carried her, back in May, it had been because he had wanted her.

Not last night, though.

Damn. And now she had the embarrassing morning-after thing to get through.

'You look better. You looked shattered last night.'

Oh, the compliments were flying today. 'I was,' she said, sliding into bed beside him and wondering how quickly she could drink her tea and get out of this humiliating situation.

'What time do you have to be at work?'

'Eight-thirty.'

'It's only ten to six. I don't have to leave till seven.'

It could have been a simple statement of fact, but there was something in his voice, something warm and gentle and coaxing, and she risked a glance at him and saw he was looking at her with a question in his eyes.

She swallowed, and put her tea down untouched. 'Ben—'

'Come here.'

So she lay down, and rested her head on his chest, and his arm closed around her back, his free hand lifting her chin gently and tilting her head back so he could see into her eyes. 'I want to make love to you, Lucy,' he said softly, and she felt her eyes fill with tears.

'Really?'

He gave a strangled laugh. 'Really. Really, really really—if it's what you want?'

'Oh, yes, please,' she whispered, and with a ragged sigh he rolled towards her, his mouth meeting hers hungrily. His hand ran down her body, his fingers splayed over her hip, her abdomen, up over her ribs, under the T-shirt and cupped her breast with a groan. He pushed the T-shirt impatiently out of the way, then stared down at her, swallowing hard.

'Your nipples are darker than they were. Like chocolate.'

And lowering his head, he took one into his mouth, rolling the other between finger and thumb, just gently, as if he knew how sensitive they'd be, and then his mouth moved on, feathering kisses over the baby, murmuring 'Good morning' on the way past, so she could feel the puff of his breath and hear the smile in his voice, and then he lifted his head.

'I hope you don't wear these outrageous knickers for your antenatal checks,' he murmured, and, slipping a finger under the elastic, he eased them down, tapping her bottom so she'd lift it and he could slide them free.

'Better,' he said, bending his head and kissing her tummy once again. And then his mouth travelled lower, the devastating accuracy of his caress robbing her limbs of control and stealing her breath.

'Ben!' she screamed, and he shifted, stripping the little scrap of lace away from her feet, ripping off his boxers, rolling to his side and taking her with him, leaving her in no doubt about his need of her.

He was so gentle, so careful, but his touch drove her crazy, his hand never leaving her, taking her over the edge in a blinding climax that left her shaken to her core.

Dimly, she was aware of his body stiffening, the ragged cry, the long, slow shudder of his release, and then his hand, trembling, cupping her face, cradling her head as he leant forward and kissed her long and slow before folding her against his still pounding heart.

She felt the baby move, felt his hand splay over it in a gentle caress, and the tears welled in her eyes.

'Are you OK?'

She nodded, squeezing her lids tightly shut, but his fingers caught her chin and lifted it. 'Look at me,' he murmured, and she made herself open her eyes and meet his, so blue, so gentle, yet still smouldering with the last embers of passion.

'You're beautiful,' he whispered. 'So beautiful. I wish I didn't have to go to work.'

'Don't worry. I have to go to work, too.'

'I know.'

He leant forward and kissed her again, softly, lingeringly, then with a sigh he rolled away, threw back the quilt and stood up, walking unselfconsciously into the *en suite* shower room and turning on the water.

He left the door open, and she sat up in bed and drank her now tepid tea. She watched Ben through the steamy glass of the cubicle door and wondered how she could ever reconcile her father to the fact that the man he was convinced had caused the death of his wife was the man she loved.

Because, she realised, she did love him. She'd loved him for years, ever since they'd worked together, and if her mother hadn't died, they might well have been together since that time.

But now it was all the most awful mess, and she had no idea where they could go from here.

'I'll see you later,' he said, shrugging into his jacket and picking up his briefcase. 'What time do you finish work?'

'Six—but, Ben, I don't know…'

'Don't know?'

'If it's a good idea.'

He stared at her, then rammed a hand through his hair,

rumpling the still damp strands and muttering something in-audible under his breath.

'Look, I'll call you,' he said after a moment. 'You drive carefully.'

'You, too.'

He gave her a fleeting smile, hesitated and came back to where she was perched on the third step and pressed a quick, hard kiss on her lips. 'Love you,' he said, and went out, leaving her open-mouthed and speechless.

'He didn't mean it,' she told the empty hall when she could speak. 'He was just saying it. Figure of speech. Nothing more. Don't read anything into it.'

But she couldn't help the crazy, irrational joy that filled her heart. She tucked it away, a warm, cosy glow to keep her going for the rest of the day…

'Morning, Lucy. Good time last night?'

She fought down a blush and smiled at her father. 'Morning, Dad. Yes, thanks.' Good? Try amazing. Incredible.

Love you.

Oh, more than amazing.

'So how did it go with Carter?'

'Car— Oh, the meeting? Fine. Very useful. Dragan couldn't make it but I'm going to fill him in later. How was the house?' she added, hoping to distract him.

'Fine. All done. So, er, where did you say you spent the night?'

Sly old fox. 'I didn't,' she said to make the point, 'but it was late by the time we'd finished dinner and I was falling asleep, so I stayed over,' she said, crossing her fingers under the edge of the desk. To her relief, Kate passed the door and stopped.

'Morning, Lucy. Nick, I wonder if I could have a word? There's a letter here from the PCT that really needs your urgent attention.'

'Oh. Sure.' He turned away.

Lucy met Kate's eyes gratefully over his shoulder and mouthed, 'Thank you.'

Kate just smiled and escorted him away, and Lucy closed the door with a sigh of relief. It dawned on her that if Kate knew the baby was Ben's and was on her side, she could make life a great deal easier. But, then, she'd thought yesterday that Dragan knew, too. And Marco? The smouldering, passionate Italian? He knew about love, although his own marriage was up the creek. Would he see the love for Ben in her eyes and know?

Which only left the reception and nursing staff and her father. And if they talked—

Her phone rang, and she lifted the receiver, banishing the little flutter of panic. 'Hello?'

'Your first patient's here, Lucy, and Toby Penhaligan's just come in—he thinks he's broken his arm. Are you free to see him?'

'Sure. I'll do that first. I'll come out,' she said.

Toby was a local fisherman, a good-looking young man in his twenties, and it wasn't the first time she'd treated him or another member of his family. He was standing in Reception, still in his oilskins and cradling one arm in the other hand. 'Hi, Doc. Sorry about this. Stupid of me—caught my toe on something and went down on deck. I thought I was OK, but I've got no strength in my arm at all and Dad reckons I've broken it.'

'Let's have a look,' she said, and led him up to the MIU.

'Toby, can you get your oilies off? Don't want to go cutting your jacket if we can avoid it, do we?' she said.

He shrugged the good arm out of the jacket and with her help he gritted his teeth and eased the coat down over his hand. By the time she'd sat him down his face was colourless and he was grim-lipped and silent. There was nothing obvious about the arm, now she could see it, and his hand was warm with good capillary refill, but he was cradling the forearm ultra-cautiously in his other hand and she'd bet her life the radius was broken, and probably the ulna as well.

'Can you squeeze my fingers?' she asked, and he tried, but he wouldn't have crumpled a tissue with that much pressure.

'Right. Can you feel your fingers?'

'Can feel the whole darned thing,' he said in disgust. 'It hurts like a proper cow. Dad's right, isn't he? It's broken.'

'I'm afraid it almost certainly is. I'll put a splint on it just to get you to hospital a bit more comfortably, but you'll have to go to St Piran and get a cast on it.'

'Pity you can't do that here.'

'It is, and we're working on it, but it'll be a while yet, Toby. Sorry.' She smiled apologetically at him, wrapped his arm in wadding and taped it to a flat support. 'There. That should stop it moving around too much until you get to St Piran. Rest it on a pillow or a cushion on your lap for the journey. And when you get there, if you see Mr Carter, can you ask him to give me a ring and let me know how it is?'

'Sure. Thanks, Doc. It'll be a while yet. Dad's got the fish to unload and if he doesn't get it away soon he'll miss the market.'

'Well, don't leave it too long. Can't you get someone else to give you a lift?'

He shook his head. 'They've all got things to do—boats

to clean down, nets to repair. Nobody's got time to run about after me. I could take the bus.'

'Not with a fracture. You could call an ambulance.'

'What, and waste their time? No, Doc, it was my own fault. I'll wait for my dad.' He stood up. 'I'll give Mr Carter your message,' he said, opening the door, and typically her father was just outside.

'What message?' he asked, stepping through the door after Toby had gone out and scowling.

'What?' she asked, pretending ignorance.

'For Ben Carter.'

'Oh. About Toby's fracture. I think it's exactly the sort of thing we could treat here—I wanted his opinion. It's really difficult for Toby to get to St Piran. He won't call an ambulance because of the waste of resources, and his father can't leave till they've unloaded the fish and got them away. And they've been out all night and they're exhausted. X-ray and plaster facilities here would improve things so much for people like him.' She smiled at him and kissed his cheek. 'And now, if you'll excuse me, I've got a full surgery and I'm already running late.'

He grunted, gave her a fleeting hug—the first for how long?—and opened the door for her. She gave a quick sigh of relief, went back down to her consulting room and carried on with her work.

CHAPTER FIVE

'LUCY?'

'Ben—hi. I take it you've seen Toby Penhaligan?' Her voice was light, as if she was pleased to hear from him. He hadn't been sure how she'd react once she'd had time to think about last night, but at least she wasn't cool and distant, and he felt a surge of something he couldn't quite analyse. Relief? No, more than that…

'Yes. He had a simple undisplaced fracture of both radius and ulna. Were you worried about him, or thinking you could have treated him there with the right facilities?'

'Oh, the latter. I thought he seemed just the sort of case I was talking about, and it was so frustrating that I had to send him to you.'

'Absolutely. You know he did it yesterday, don't you? But they were out all night and couldn't get back until they'd hauled in the lines.'

'And his father couldn't bring him to you till the fish were unloaded and away, or they would have lost their money for the catch. It's a tough life for our fishermen, and I wouldn't want to be doing it in those rough seas, I'm not good on the water,' she said, and then went on with a slightly self-conscious laugh, 'That's by the by. I wanted to know—so I can use it in an argument with the powers that be—what time he arrived, when he was seen and how long it took, so I can compare it to what would have happened if I could have put a cast on it when I saw him at eight forty-five this morning.'

Of course she did. All business. Ben forced himself to stop thinking about the sound of her voice and concentrate on her words. 'Let me check the notes. Right, he arrived at the department at ten-fifty, was seen by the triage nurse and sent to wait until eleven twenty-five, then he was seen by one of the doctors, X-rayed and then a cast put on it at twelve-ten. He was discharged from the department at twelve forty-two. I got the staff to log it because I knew you'd want to know.'

He could hear the smile in her voice. 'You're a regular sweetheart,' she said, then went on in a more businesslike tone, 'So he had a wait for the doctor, a wait for X-ray, a wait for the doctor to confirm the diagnosis and a wait for the cast. And it took one hour fifty-two minutes.'

'Yup. Which is pretty good for here. And then there's the travelling time and parking—say another hour to an hour and a half.'

'Three hours, then, on a good day, not to mention the added discomfort of the journey.'

'And you could have done it in—what? Forty-five minutes?'

'Something like that,' she agreed. 'So he would have been out of here and on his way home by nine-thirty, instead of one-thirty—four hours earlier—and his father wouldn't have been taken away from his work. And, of course, if one of the nurses was trained to take X-rays, it would cut down the time I or one of the other doctors would be tied up as well. That's fantastic. Thank you so much for all that information.'

'My pleasure. I wasn't sure if I'd catch you, actually,' he added, trying to sound casual. 'I thought you might have gone home for lunch.'

'No, Kate nipped out and bought us all sandwiches from the bakery. I'm just eating them now.'

'Are you alone?'

'Yes. I'm in my consulting room.'

'So—about tonight,' he murmured, trying very hard not to think about what they'd done that morning and how very, very much he wanted to do it again. 'How about supper?'

There was a slight pause, and his heart sank. She's going to say no, he thought, but then she said, 'That would be lovely, but can we make it early? I'm really tired. I could do with getting back for an early night.'

His heart, on the way up, sank again, but he told himself not to be selfish. She was pregnant. She needed her rest. 'Good idea,' the doctor and father in him said. 'So are you coming to me, or shall I bring something to you, or are we ready to go public?'

She laughed softly. 'You think coming to me isn't going public? Dream on, Ben. This is Penhally.'

Of course. 'So—where, then?'

'Yours?'

'Sure,' he said, disappointed that he didn't get to take her out and spoil her, but glad that he'd be seeing her anyway. 'Want me to pick you up, or would you rather drive yourself?'

'I'll drive. Shall I come over as soon as I've finished?'

'Good idea. Anything you particularly fancy?'

'Fish,' she said promptly. 'Sea bass. There are some in the fridge here, courtesy of the Penhaligans. Shall I bring two?'

'That would be good. And I'll make you something irresistible for pudding.'

She chuckled, and the sound did amazing things to his nerve endings. 'Chocolate,' she ordered, and he laughed.

'How did I guess?' There was a tap on his door and his specialist registrar stuck her head round it. Ben lifted a hand to keep her there. 'Lucy, I'm sorry, I have to go now, but I'll see you later,' he said, and replaced the phone on its cradle. 'Jo, thanks for coming by. I've got an appointment at two-thirty. It's only a few minutes away—fifteen at the most. Can you hold the fort?'

'Sure. It's pretty quiet at the moment.'

'Don't say that,' he warned, and glanced at his watch. Five to two. Just time to catch up on some paperwork before he had to leave.

So this was it. Tregorran House, Lucy's grandmother's family home and the house of her dreams. Ben walked slowly up to the open back door and called out, and a young man in a suit appeared and strode towards him, hand outstretched.

'Mr Carter? Come on in.'

He shook hands and went into what seemed to be a lean-to scullery or boot room, and through to the dirty and desperately dated kitchen. 'Sorry about the back door, the front door won't open,' the agent was saying. 'They're never used in this part of the world, and the key seems to have gone missing. It's a shame because it's a lovely way in and out, you get to see the views from there. Come on through and have a look around.'

It was smaller than he'd expected. Low ceilings, but here and there were old oak beams that hinted at a concealed structure crying out to be revealed. There was a huge granite inglenook in the kitchen, an ancient and filthy cream Aga fitting easily into the space once occupied by the range, and smaller, more functional granite fireplaces in the two living rooms that bracketed the front door. The rooms weren't huge, but they were cosy, overlooking the garden, and he could imagine them with fires crackling in the grates.

Upstairs the fireplaces were boarded over, but he'd bet his bottom dollar there were pretty little cast-iron grates behind the boards, or there had been in the past.

But the outstanding thing about the whole property, once you got over the poor state of the decor and the fact that it clearly needed a serious cash injection, was the view. All the principal rooms faced west, looking down the coast towards the Atlantic Ocean, and the sunsets Lucy loved would be spectacular.

'Does it go down to the beach?' he asked, and the agent shook his head.

'No. The plot's quite small, just the half acre of garden the house sits in, but there isn't really a beach here anyway, just a pile of rocks. You can get to the beach about half a mile away over the fields, though. They're owned by the neighbouring farmer. It's a lovely little cove and there's quite a good road to it, too. It's very pretty, and the path's well maintained—it's part of the Cornish Coastal Path—but, no, it hasn't got beach access. Otherwise the guide price would be a great deal higher. There's nothing the London buyers like more than their own private beach. And, of course, because the planners have ruled out any development of the site other than extension of the existing house within the realms of permitted development, that's also going to keep the price a bit more accessible. That said, we've had quite a keen interest in the property,' he added, as if he was worried he'd put Ben off. Or was it agent-speak for 'This is highly sought after and you'd be foolish to miss it'?

Maybe.

Whatever, it was irrelevant to Ben. The house was awful at the moment, dingy and rundown and outdated, but it had the potential to be a lovely cosy family home, and it was Lucy's dream. If he could get it for her without bankrupting himself into the hereafter, he'd do it.

'I'm sorry to rush you, but I've got another viewing to get to. Could I leave you to go around the outside on your own?' the agent asked, and Ben nodded.

'Of course. I've seen all I need to.' More than enough to make up his mind.

He spent a few minutes looking around the outside, checking out the structure and exploring the rundown and tangled garden that Lucy obviously remembered through rose-tinted specs, and then he headed back to the hospital.

To his relief Jo had coped without him, and it was still quiet, so he shut himself away in his office and rang his solicitor.

'What's the procedure for buying a house at auction?' he asked. 'Because I want you to do it for me. Friday, two o'clock, Tregorran House. And I don't want to take any chances.'

'Ah, Lucy. Got time for a chat?'

'Dragan—hi. I've been meaning to catch up with you.' She sat back in her chair and stretched out the kinks in her neck. 'How's Melinda?'

'Oh, fine. Thank you both so much for sorting her arm out.'

'Pleasure—well, hardly, but you know what I mean,' she said with a laugh. 'I'm sorry you missed our meeting. How's the dog?'

He smiled. 'Really sweet. She's got a broken leg and a

huge laceration on her side, but nobody's come forward yet to report her missing. Melinda's set the leg and she's looking after her for now.'

'No more biting?'

He shook his head and smiled again. 'No. She's a sweetheart. She was just scared. Anyway, this meeting...'

'Yes—really useful. Ben thinks we could do it. If we could build on out the back as we'd discussed, then he thinks it'll be fine. Maybe reorganise upstairs a bit and have downstairs as a fracture clinic, essentially.' She ran through the key points of their discussion. Dragan nodded at intervals, and then she sat back and stretched again and sighed.

'You OK?'

'Oh, Dragan, I'm so tired. Just the thought of another six or eight weeks before I can give up is enough to send me to sleep!'

He frowned in concern. 'Lucy, you shouldn't be overdoing it. You should be resting now. We can manage.'

'You're sounding like my father,' she pointed out, and he gave an embarrassed laugh and sat back.

'OK, it's not my job, but I care about you. We all do.'

She flapped her hand at him, touched but still not having any of it. 'I'm fine. I think we ought to have a meeting. Kate was talking about setting something up with the local NHS trust architect and Ben here on site, but Dad's so anti.'

'Don't worry about him, Lucy. He wants what's best for the patients.'

'He's just so blinkered,' she said, thinking not only of the forthcoming meeting but also of the news she yet had to give her father—news that couldn't possibly make the situation any easier.

'I take it he doesn't know?'

She jerked her head up and met his eyes, her mouth already opening to deny everything, and saw the gentle understanding in Dragan's eyes. She swallowed and looked away. 'No. He doesn't know.'

'That will be hard.'

'It will be impossible,' she said softly, 'but it has to be done.' She sucked in a breath and straightened up. 'Right, I have to get on. I've got a clinic in a minute. If you let Kate know when you're free for this meeting, she'll try and organise it.'

'I'll do that,' he said, and got to his feet, then hesitated. 'Lucy, if there's anything I can do…?'

He left it hanging, and with a fleeting smile he went out. He was so kind and thoughtful. So was Marco. The two of them fussed over her like a couple of clucky old hens. It was only her father she had a problem with.

And she was going to have to deal with it.

Ben cooked the sea bass beautifully.

Outside, on a charcoal barbeque with the lid shut, in the bleak and windy garden, and then brought them into the house with the skin lightly charred and the inside meltingly tender. He'd prepared a green salad and hot jacket potatoes, and then he produced the wickedest hot chocolate sauce pudding she'd ever seen in her life.

'It's a fabulously easy recipe—my mother taught it to me,' he said with a grin, and put a big dollop of it on a plate and handed it to her. 'Here, you need this,' he said, and gave her a dish of clotted cream.

'Define need,' she said wryly, and he chuckled.

'You have to have some treats. Anyway, it's probably full of vitamin D.'

'You don't have to talk me into it,' she said, plopping a generous spoonful onto the top of the chocolate goo and then tasting it.

'Mmm,' she said, and then didn't talk any more for a few gorgeous, tastebud-melting minutes. Conversation would have been sacrilege.

'Good?' he asked when she'd all but scraped the glaze off the plate, and she laughed and pushed the plate away and arched back, giving her stomach room.

'Fabulous,' she said emphatically. 'Assuming I don't just burst. Thank you.'

'My pleasure. Coffee?'

'Mmm—thanks. Can I help wash up?'

'No—the dishwasher'll do it all. You can go and sit down in the sitting room and put your feet up.'

'Is that an order?' she asked, and he tipped his head on one side and studied her closely.

'That's a loaded question,' he retorted after a moment, a grin tugging at one corner of his mouth. 'I don't think I'll answer it.'

Chuckling to herself, she went into the sitting room and curled up on the sofa, not because he'd told her to but because she wanted to anyway. She'd had a busy day, starting with Tony Penhaligan and ending with an overrunning surgery, and she'd hardly had a minute to herself in between. So she was more than happy to sit down, and after a moment she stretched her legs out, rested her head back and closed her eyes.

There was a gorgeous smell of fresh coffee drifting from the kitchen, and she sniffed it appreciatively. It would set off the chocolate pud to perfection. She heard him come in, heard him set the tray down and felt the end of the sofa dip under his weight.

'White, no sugar,' she murmured, and he chuckled and rubbed her feet affectionately before pouring the coffee.

'Here—sit up and open your eyes,' he said, and she did as she was told, watching him over the rim of the mug as she sipped it.

'Thank you for cooking for me,' she said, wriggling her toes under his thigh.

He smiled. 'My pleasure. Thank you for the sea bass.'

'I'll pass it on to the Penhaligans. Good day?'

His eyes flicked away, his attention turning to his coffee. 'Yes. Very good. Busy. How about you?'

'Oh, busy, too. I phoned you during the afternoon to try and set up a time for this next meeting with the architect, but they said you were out of the department.'

'Mmm—I had a meeting,' he said, but he didn't elaborate. Not that he had to tell her everything about his life, of course he didn't, and if he started poking about in her life she'd be less than impressed, but somehow she felt excluded, and she didn't like it. She wanted, she realised with some surprise, to be entitled to know who he'd met with and why. Probably someone on the hospital management committee, the chief exec or something, nothing interesting at all—but it would have been nice if he'd told her, or if she'd had the right to ask.

Which was just plain silly. They hardly knew each other. Just because they had an unfortunate tendency to end up in bed every time they met, it didn't mean they were part of each other's lives!

And then he said, 'Stay with me tonight,' and she felt an overwhelming urge to do just that. To go to bed with him, to curl up in his arms and sleep, just as she had last night. She hadn't slept so well in ages, but she couldn't let herself be lured into it so readily. It would be all to easy to let it become a habit, and until her father knew…

'I can't,' she said, with genuine regret, and he sighed and smiled ruefully.

'I knew you'd say that.'

'It's just…'

'Difficult? I know. Lucy, if you want me there when you tell him—'

'No!' she said quickly, sitting up so fast she nearly slopped her coffee. 'No,' she said again, more calmly this time. 'I just need to find the right moment.'

He nodded, then looked down at her feet, giving them undue attention. 'I do love you, you know. I wasn't just saying it this morning.'

She put the coffee down, very carefully, on the table that was conveniently in reach, and stared at him. 'You do? But you hardly know me.'

'Rubbish. You haven't changed. We spent six months together when you were on your A and E rotation.'

'And you had a girlfriend!'

'Not for all of it. I ended it because she wasn't what I wanted. I hadn't known that until I met someone who was, and then it gradually dawned on me that I was with the wrong woman. And because I wanted to be sure, I gave us time, because I felt that this could really be it—the once-in-a-lifetime thing. Then you got to the end of your rotation, and shortly after that—'

He broke off and looked away again, and she finished for him, 'My mother died, and it all went horribly wrong.'

He nodded, and for a moment neither of them spoke, then she said softly, 'Ben, what if I've changed? What if I'm not the woman you think I am? What if time's altered your perception of me and I can't live up to your mental image?' She swallowed, facing her fears head on. 'And what if you don't live up to mine?'

He glanced over, a quick frown pleating his brow, and he searched her face. 'So we'll take it slowly,' he suggested at last. 'Give ourselves time to get to know the people we are now. But to do that, we need to spend time together, so we have to find a way to do that.'

She nodded, knowing he was right. Marriage was for life, as the saying went, not just for Christmas, and she wasn't sure if they knew each other well enough yet for such a huge commitment. But if everything was right between them by then, she'd much rather they were married when the baby was born, old-fashioned though it might be. Some things, she thought, were meant to be old-fashioned. And if they were to get to know each other, they had to spend time together, despite her father complicating the issue.

'This weekend?' she suggested. 'I'm off from Friday after my morning surgery until Monday morning.'

'Sure. That would be good. I'm on call tomorrow night, but I've got the afternoon off on Friday. I've got things to do but we could meet up when I'm done. I'll book us a table somewhere for dinner on Friday night—perhaps in Padstow—and then we can come back here and chill for a couple of days. Go for a walk, toast crumpets, whatever—what do you think?'

She nodded again, even the thought enough to make her

feel more relaxed. 'Sounds blissful,' she said with a smile. 'And now I really ought to go home so I don't fall asleep at the wheel.'

Or succumb to the seductive charm of those gorgeous blue eyes…

He helped her up, held her coat for her, tucked it around her to keep her warm and kissed her lingeringly before waving her off, then went back inside.

What if I can't live up to your mental image? And what if you don't live up to mine?

He felt a tense knot of something strangely like fear in his chest. Please, God, by the weekend he'd have something good to tell her. Something that hopefully would help a little with the mental image she had of him?

Oh, hell. What if it didn't? What if it was just nostalgia for the house and not a real urge to live there? And what if he didn't get the house after all? What if, despite all his preparation, despite getting the money sorted, pinning his purchaser down to a date, getting his solicitor to bid for him over the phone and sort out the paperwork—what if, despite all that, he was quite simply outbid at the auction? If the price just went up and up and up until it was out of his reach?

Lucy stared out of her consulting-room window across the car park to the sea beyond the harbour wall, her emotions torn.

He loved her. He'd said it as if he really meant it, not in a moment of passion, not as a passing farewell like before, but quietly, thoughtfully.

And she so, so wanted to believe him, but there was a bit of her that was afraid he was talking himself into it because of the baby. Because he wanted to create the image of the perfect family, and that was the first step, the cornerstone.

Maybe he genuinely believed he did love her, but she was too scared to believe it.

Her phone rang, and it was Hazel, the head receptionist, to tell her that her first patient had arrived. Even the thought exhausted her. She'd been busy yesterday, and no doubt today would be the same. She hoped not, because otherwise she'd be too tired by tomorrow to enjoy her long weekend with Ben. But putting it off any longer wouldn't make it go away.

As she'd expected, the day was hellish, and she fell into bed exhausted at eight o'clock. She heard the phone ring in the sitting room, but she'd forgotten to bring it into her bedroom because she wasn't on call, and by the time she'd decided she ought to get up, it had stopped ringing.

Oh, well, if it was important they'd ring again, she thought, but whoever it was didn't. She could dial 1471 and check, she thought, or see if there was a message.

She fell asleep again, then had to get up in the night because the baby was wriggling around on her bladder, and on her way back to bed she checked the answering-machine and found a message from Ben.

Damn. She should have got out of bed and taken the call, and really wished she had. She played the message, sitting in bed with the phone, listening to his voice and wishing she was with him.

She played it again. 'You aren't there, or maybe you're having an early night. It's not important. I just wanted to talk to you. It seems odd not seeing you two nights running. Take care. I'll see you tomorrow.' Then a pause, then, 'Love you.'

She looked at her bedside clock. Two-thirty in the morning—too late, or too early, to ring. Except he was on call—so either he was working or he would be asleep. Either way, she couldn't really disturb him, and he wouldn't ring again.

She sent a text to his mobile.

'Thanks for message. Early night. Looking forward to w/e. Lucy.' And then, for good measure, 'X'. She nearly put 'Love you' like he had, but it seemed too massively important to risk getting it wrong, and when she did tell him, if she ever did, she wanted to see his face.

Suddenly the afternoon seemed much, much too far away…

Ben didn't want to be at the auction.

He wasn't sure if Nick Tremayne would be there, but he didn't want to risk it. He didn't know how the man would feel about him buying the house, but frankly he didn't care. This wasn't about Nick, it was about Lucy, and if he'd thought enough of the place to hold on to it for several years, then once he and his daughter had sorted out this glitch in their relationship, Ben was sure that keeping the house in the family could only be good for all of them.

But Lucy was his primary concern, and he had so much riding on it he felt sick.

He'd booked the time off, but now he wished he hadn't. He couldn't go home and sit there, though, just waiting for the phone to ring, so he drove to the house. Well, almost. He didn't want to push his luck, tempt fate, whatever. So he sat in the car, just down the lane, and rang his solicitor.

He got his secretary, and asked her to get him to ring as soon as there was any news.

'I'll call you on another line,' she promised, 'while Simon's bidding—that way he can talk to you at the same time, give you a chance to decide how you want to play it.'

He felt the tension ratchet up a notch. 'OK. I'll keep the phone free,' he promised, and plugged in the charger. He wasn't going to lose the house because of something stupid like a flat battery.

There was a woman up on the headland, leaning into the wind, her clothes plastered against her body and her hair streaming out behind like a figurehead on an old sailing ship. Except—this figurehead was pregnant. *Lucy?* Yes, Lucy—standing there, keeping vigil, saying goodbye while the house was sold out from under her.

Well, hardly, because she didn't live there, but emotionally it must feel like that, he realised, and he felt the tension ratchet up yet again. He *had* to get it.

The phone rang, startling him, and he grabbed it.

'Ben—it's Simon. We're on. I've got the auctioneer on hands-free so you can listen in and talk to me at the same time.'

'Great.'

Except it wasn't great, it was terrifying, and he realised that even in the grip of a major accident, when the hospital instituted its MAJAX plan, he'd never felt quite this scared that things would go wrong.

He could hear the bidding, hear the figures rising perilously close to his maximum. He'd still got the budget for the work in hand, but it needed that. He couldn't use it all, but he could dip into it if he had to—

'Ben?'

'Another five thousand—in ones,' he instructed, and listened as the price climbed slowly up, long pauses now between the bids.

'The other bidder's only gone up five hundred—he must be close to his limit,' Simon said.

'Call his bluff. Go up five thousand more, in one jump,' Ben said, his heart pounding. 'See if you can knock him out.'

There was a long, long silence, then he heard the auctioneer say, 'Going once… Going twice…' and the sound of the hammer coming down. But who—?

'Congratulations!' Simon said. 'You've got yourself a house.'

Somehow Ben ended the call. He wasn't sure what he'd said, what he'd agreed to do. It didn't matter. He'd call Simon back later. For now there was a woman standing on the headland, and she needed his attention.

He drove up to the house—his house, or it would be soon—and turned in the gate. Her car was there, pulled up by the door, and he blocked her in just in case he missed her somehow.

He didn't. She was still there, standing staring out to sea, and he went down the track by the side of the garden, across the field and walked up behind her.

'Lucy?'

She turned slowly, and he could see the tears on her cheeks, dried by the wind.

'It's gone,' she said woodenly. 'The house. It's gone. The sale was at two.'

'I know.'

She hugged herself, her hands wrapping around her slender arms and hanging on, and he stood between her and the biting wind and cupped her face in his hands.

'I've got something for you,' he said softly. 'Come back to the house with me.'

Her brow furrowed. 'The house?'

'Mmm.'

She turned, and he put his arm round her and led her carefully back over the field. At the gateway to the house he stopped and scooped her into his arms.

'What are you doing?' she asked, startled.

'It's tradition,' he said, 'except it should be the front door, but I can't do that because I haven't got the keys and anyway the front door key's missing.'

She stared at him blankly. 'Tradition?'

'To carry your woman over the threshold.' He took a deep breath and walked through the gateway. 'Welcome to your new home, Lucy.'

She stared at him for an age, then hope flickered in her eyes. 'My new…?'

'I bought the house—for you,' he told her gently, and she burst into tears.

CHAPTER SIX

SHE couldn't believe it.

He'd put her down carefully on her feet, on the driveway of the house, and he was looking down at her expectantly.

No, not expectantly, exactly, but as if he wasn't quite sure what reception his news was getting, and needed—desperately needed—to know.

'Oh, Ben,' she said, flinging her arms around him and hugging him, then letting him go and looking up at him searchingly while she hunted for a tissue.

'Here,' he said, and handed her one with a smile, and she blew her nose, scrubbed away the still welling tears, and stared up at him again.

'I can't believe— How on earth did you afford it? It must have gone for a fortune. You're crazy!'

'Only a tiny fortune,' he said with a wry, slightly uncertain smile. 'I'd sold my house—never did like it—and I'd been looking for somewhere older, somewhere with character. Then you told me about this, and—well, there I was, in a position to do something about it, and I thought— Hell, I don't know what I thought, but if the chance was there to give you the house of your dreams, somewhere you'd be safe and happy, I didn't want to risk not doing it. And if you really didn't want it after all, I thought I could always stick it back on the market.'

'You really bought it for me?'

His mouth quirked into a smile again. 'Well, I was kind of hoping you'd let me share it, but—yes, I bought it for you. You and the baby.' His face shadowed. 'But it's quite isolated—apart from the farmhouse over there, you can't see another house, and it's nearly a mile to the village, if you can call it that. It seems like a pretty tiny community. If it was just nostalgia—'

'No!' she said hastily, hurrying to correct him. 'No, Ben, it wasn't just nostalgia. I *love* this house. I've always loved it. I just can't believe—' She broke off, not knowing how to continue, what to say, still utterly overwhelmed by what he'd done.

And the way he'd presented it, too, not as some kind of grand gesture, not a '*ta-da!*' but humbly, as if he'd done it to make her happy and not to score Brownie points.

'It's a shame we can't go inside, but I won't get the keys for ages.'

She dangled them under his nose. 'I got them off Dad. Said I wanted to have a last look around.' She held them out to him. 'Well, go on, then,' she said, but he shook his head.

'It's not mine yet,' he reminded her, and it was as if the mention of her father's name had taken all the colour out of the day. But he was still smiling, his eyes searching her face for clues, and suddenly she wanted to look around it with him, to tell him about her grandmother, to show him the house from her memories.

'I can take you in,' she pointed out, waggling the keys. 'I have the vendor's permission to be here.'

And taking him by the hand, she led him to the back door, opened it and then stopped him when he would have lifted her. 'No,' she said. 'Not yet. Not until we're…' She caught herself, then went on, 'Not until it's properly yours.'

What had she been going to say?

Not until we're—what?

Married?

One step at a time, he warned himself, cutting off his hopes before they got totally out of sync with reality.

He stopped worrying about it and followed her into the house, watching her face as she went from room to room, telling him stories.

'Oh, it looks so dirty and shabby, but I can remember my grandfather's coat hanging here, and my grandmother's elderly jacket that she used for the garden. Tweed, good and thick, utterly hideous, but it kept her warm. And the dogs always slept here, next to the Aga,' she said, moving through to the kitchen. 'Grannie was always baking—apple pies, cakes, wholemeal bread that was so wonderful I still haven't found anything to match it. And there was often a casserole in the bottom oven, or a baked egg custard made with milk from the house cow and eggs from the chickens that used to scratch about outside.'

'Do you want chickens?' he asked, fascinated by the emotions flitting over her face.

She laughed. 'Maybe. There was a cockerel who used to crow outside my bedroom window at some revolting hour of the morning, but I never minded because it meant I was here, and I loved it so much. Yes, chickens would be fun, but not the house cow. Too much like hard work! I remember being kicked off the milking stool by her when I was nine, and my mother wouldn't let me milk her again. Said it was too dangerous. Anyway, we can get milk from the Trevellyans down the road.'

We?

They went through to the rooms at the front, the one she'd said had been the dining room and the one with the lovely fireplace that was just crying out for a big old dog grate with fragrant apple logs burning in the hearth.

'We used to toast crumpets here by the fire,' she told him. 'And we'd butter them, and it would drip through and onto our fingers and the dogs would sneak up and lick the backs of our hands where the butter had run round. They used to get yelled at and shooed out.'

'Collies?'

'Mostly. There was a Jack Russell at one time, but he was ancient. He was allowed in here by the fire, and sometimes even on my lap. Grannie was so upset when he died.'

They went upstairs, to the rooms overlooking the sea, and she took him into the smallest one over the front door. 'This was mine. Jack and Ed shared the room at the back, and Grannie and Grandpa were in the big bedroom next door that way, and my parents were in that room.'

'Jack and Ed?'

'My brothers.' She stroked her fingers reverently over the window-sill, wide enough to sit on, and told him about how she'd sat there by the open window in the summer, after the cockerel had woken her, and waited for the dawn. 'Sometimes I saw a fox sneak past the chicken house, and once I saw one run off with a chicken in his mouth. Grannie was livid.'

She laughed, the sound like a waterfall, and he felt the tight knot of tension that had been there for days start to ease. It was going to be all right. He knew it was.

They just had that one last hurdle to get over…

'Did you know about this?'

The door crashed back against the wall, and the baby inside her stiffened, startled by the sudden noise. Lucy cradled it automatically, soothing it with her hands, and met her father's eyes with as much composure as she could muster.

She didn't pretend not to know what he was talking about. He was brandishing a letter from the estate agent, and his face was stiff with fury.

'Yes, I knew,' she said. 'Not until afterwards, though.'

'And you didn't think fit to tell me? My own daughter, and you didn't tell me that *that man* had bought my house?'

'Your mother's house,' she pointed out, and he growled under his breath and slapped the paperwork down on her desk.

'Don't split hairs, Lucy! How did you know?'

'I was there,' she told him, lifting her chin. 'At the house— saying goodbye. Ben turned up. He told me then—right after the auction. He'd bid over the phone.'

'Coward.'

'Not at all,' she said, frustrated. 'He'd been at work. He didn't have time to drive all the way to the auction house.'

'God! He only did it to spite me.'

'Don't be ridiculous, Dad. It's a lovely house. He's been looking for something for ages.'

Tell him! her conscience urged, but she bottled out in the face of his already considerable anger. Not because she was afraid of him, because she knew perfectly well how much he loved her and that he would never lift a finger to her, but because now wasn't the time. She had a surgery starting in a minute, and so did he.

And she wanted time to talk it through with him, to explain her feelings, to discuss her mother's death a little more rationally. But right now, she knew, he simply wouldn't listen.

'Well, I wanted to let it go,' he said at last. 'And maybe it's for the best. At least now I know I'll never have to go into the house again.'

And he strode out, leaving her sitting there in the ringing silence.

So much for her blissful, relaxing weekend. They'd had a wonderful time. Ben had taken her down to Padstow, to a café, one of her favourite places, where the food was fresh and unpretentious and the atmosphere lively. It wasn't romantic, but it was fun, and she'd accidentally squirted Ben with prawn juice and they'd laughed till she'd thought they'd die from lack of oxygen.

Then they'd gone back to his house and he'd made love to her on the sofa in front of the fire, and then again in the morning, lying in bed lazily until midday while he'd waited on her and indulged her every whim.

Breakfast in bed—*pain au chocolat*, gallons of delicately flavoured tea with just a touch of milk, fresh fruit sliced into a bowl and fed to her with his fingers—and then she'd sucked the juice off them, and his eyes had darkened and he'd put the bowl down, moved the tray and kissed the juice from her lips.

It had taken a very long time, Lucy remembered with a fleeting smile. In the afternoon they'd gone to the supermarket and bought crumpets, and rump steak and shoestring fries for dinner with loads of salad, and he'd cooked the chocolate pudding again.

They'd got up earlier on Sunday and gone for a lovely walk on the coastal path by Tregorran House, and then they'd gone back inside and talked about what he was going to do to the house. She'd stayed over that night as well, and had only got home this morning in time for surgery.

And now her father was baying for Ben's blood, and she didn't know what to do for the best.

She shut the door, sank down at her desk and let her hands drift down to cradle her baby. It had been such a lovely weekend, and by the end of it she'd managed to convince herself that everything would be all right.

Ben had been so good to her, and they'd had so much fun. She knew she loved him, and she was beginning to think that, yes, he really did love her, and they'd get married and live happily ever after in Tregorran House and everything would be great.

Stupid. She'd let herself get carried away on a big fluffy cloud, and now she was down to earth again with a bang.

Eight and a half weeks to go, she thought. Eight and a half weeks to convince her father that Ben was all right and he hadn't done anything wrong, and reconcile them to the point that he would give her away to Ben with his blessing, so they could get married before the baby came.

Not a chance.

If only things were more normal and they were married. So the baby could be born in wedlock.

Grief, what an old-fashioned saying. Wedlock. Like prison.

Only with Ben, she knew, it wouldn't be. It would be wonderful. But there was still the problem of her father, and getting both him and Ben at the wedding might be more than she could manage.

So could she marry Ben without her father there? She swallowed hard, blinking back tears. Without her father's knowledge?

No. She couldn't do that. It would be bad enough not having her mother there. For her father not to be there either— no. She couldn't even contemplate it.

And anyway, they were light years from that, and before she could worry about it, she had a surgery to get through, and a whole batch of visits, including one to Edith Jones. She'd tried to ring her first thing but hadn't got any reply. There could have been lots of reasons for that, not least that Edith couldn't move that fast any longer.

On the other hand—no, don't borrow trouble, she told herself, and worked her way steadily through her patients, putting Edith and Ben and her father firmly out of her mind for now.

Doris Trefussis, the practice cleaner and general all-round good egg, stuck her head round the door after her last patient had left. 'Want a cuppa, my bird?' she asked, giving Lucy a smile that still twinkled even though she was beginning to show her age. She was supposedly fifty-nine, but by all accounts she'd been fifty-nine for years. Thin, wiry and always smiling, Lucy didn't know what they'd do without her.

'No, I'm fine, Doris, thank you. I've got to go out on my visits. I'm a bit worried about Edith Jones—she's not answering her phone.'

'Saw her yesterday out in her garden—she looked all right,' Doris said. 'Can't you have a little drink first?'

Lucy smiled but still shook her head. 'No. You can make me one when I get back. And if you've got a minute, you couldn't slip round to the bakery and pick up a sandwich, could you? Wholemeal bread, something healthy without too much mayo?'

'Of course, dear. I'll get one with a nice bit of chicken in it—easily digestible. And a little apple turnover—I know you love them.'

'You spoil me,' she said, giving Doris the money and wondering how huge she was going to be by the time everyone, including Ben, had finished feeding her up. 'Right, I'm off to Mrs Jones. I'll see you later. Bless you.'

She drove to Edith's first, a little bungalow high up above the old town, in a development characterised by its lack of any architectural merit but a comfortable, friendly community for all that. Edith and her husband had lived there all their married lives, and Lucy sincerely hoped Edith could continue to live there for ever. She'd certainly have support from her neighbours. She'd known most of them for years and years.

She pulled up on the road outside and looked around, seeing nothing out of the way. Nothing to indicate that there was a problem, certainly. Getting her bag out of the car, she went up to the front door and rang the bell, listening carefully.

Odd. The television wasn't on. It always was. Perhaps she'd gone away—spent the weekend with one of her children and not got back yet, perhaps? Except Doris had seen her yesterday, out in the garden. She rang the bell again, and bent down and peered through the letter box.

'Mrs Jones?' she called. 'Edith? It's Dr Lucy. Are you all right?'

Silence, and then, just as she let the flap go, she heard a faint cry. She pushed it open again. 'Edith? Are you there?'

'In the kitchen—key under the pot,' Edith called weakly.

Pot? Which pot? There were hundreds, in all shapes and

sizes, clustered around the front door. She checked under all the obvious ones, then went round to the back door and tried there, and to her relief there it was under the first pot she lifted—a shiny silver key. She opened the door and went straight into the kitchen, and found Edith lying awkwardly on the floor, propped up against the kitchen cupboards where she'd hauled herself.

'Edith!' she exclaimed softly, crouching down beside her a little awkwardly and touching her cheek in a gesture of reassurance.

'Oh, Dr Lucy, I'm so glad to see you. I knew you were coming—it's the only thing that's kept me going. I heard the phone ring and ring, and I just couldn't get to it. I was so hoping you'd come—not just think I was out.'

Lucy felt a huge wave of relief that she hadn't, in fact done that. She knew many doctors would have, but people in this tight-knit community didn't let each other down, and if Edith hadn't been going to be there, she would have told her.

'Don't move. Let me check you over. You just stay there. Let me get you a pillow for your head and something to tuck behind your back.' She ran into the bedroom, came back with a pair of pillows and the quilt off the bed and, after checking that Edith wasn't experiencing any back pain, she slid the pillows into place and then ran her hands gently over all her limbs.

'Oh!' Edith cried when Lucy touched her left leg. 'Oh, that's so sore. I think I landed on my knee—I must have tripped over the cat, I think.'

Possibly. There was no sign of a cat, but Lucy was much more worried about Edith. The knee was hugely swollen, a dark purple bruise fanning out from the centre of her kneecap, and she wouldn't have been surprised to learn it was a starburst fracture. 'Any idea how long ago you fell, my love?' she asked gently, her eyes still scanning over the damaged leg.

'Hours.'

Hmm. Edith was breathless, obviously in pain, and Lucy knew the first step was to get her over to St Piran and get her checked out. 'I'm going to call an ambulance and get them to take you to the hospital to get this knee looked at,' she said, and it was a measure of how serious the pain was that Edith, stubborn and independent as she was, didn't argue.

Once she'd called the ambulance service, Lucy tucked the quilt around her and gave her pain relief, hooked her up to the portable oxygen and sat back to wait, holding Edith's hand. It didn't take long. Paramedic Maggie Pascoe, a familiar face not only to Lucy from her time in the emergency department at St Piran but also to Edith, as she was a local girl, came running up the path to the door, and Lucy quickly let her in.

'You're lucky, we were just parked up the road having our lunch,' she said with a smile. 'Hello, Edith—what have you done to yourself, you silly thing?'

'Oh, I know—so stupid. I just fell. And I think I've wet myself,' Edith added in distress, as Lucy handed over to Maggie.

'Don't worry, my love, we'll soon sort you out,' Maggie said with a smile, and they quickly loaded her onto the trolley and trundled her down the hall. The path from the door was mercifully flat and straight, and Lucy had given her enough pain relief to make the journey bearable.

'My cat!' she called, just as they were about to close the doors. 'Don't forget my cat! Sarah Pearce will feed it—number 12. She knows about the key.'

'I'll tell her—don't worry.'

Lucy watched them go, closed up the house, put the key back under the pot and went round to see Sarah Pearce, filling her in quickly, then she got back into her car out of the wind and phoned Ben.

'Lucy, hi. Are you all right?'

'I'm fine. I'm sending a patient to you—Edith Jones. She's had a heavy fall in the kitchen and hit her knee on the corner of a cupboard, by the look of it. Might have a starburst fracture, but she's also wet herself. It might be nothing, but she has congestive heart failure and occasional irregularities of her heart rhythm. Might be worth checking it out to make sure she didn't have a little stroke or TIA. No other symptoms apart from breathlessness. She's on her way.'

'OK, I'll look out for her. Thanks. Um—I had a call from your father.'

She felt a chill run over her. 'About the house?'

'Mmm. He's not pleased.'

'No, I know. He came in this morning and had a go—then he ended by saying it was just as well, he wanted a clean break with the house and at least he'd never have to go in it again.'

She felt a sob welling in her chest, and clamped her lips together to stop it coming out, but Ben must have heard something, because his voice was concerned. 'Lucy, don't,' he said softly. 'Oh, my love, I'm so sorry. I thought I was helping you. I didn't want to make it worse.'

'No, you haven't,' she said quickly. 'It's just me. It's hormones. I'm just feeling sentimental and I want everything to be perfect and it isn't. Ignore me. Look out for Edith. I'll speak to you later.'

'OK. Take care. Love you.'

She opened her mouth, shut it again, then said, 'You, too. I'll see you later.'

You, too, what?

You, too, take care? Or, I love you, too?

Ben stared at the phone, put the receiver down softly and stood there for a second. How long could this go on? How long could Nick continue to persecute his daughter because of his stiff-necked reluctance to accept the facts?

He paused beside Resus. The room was empty, but in his mind's eye he could see Annabel lying there, blood everywhere, and Nick's agonised face as he realised that his wife's life was slipping away and there was nothing anyone could do to save her.

He'd struggled and fought to get to her, had needed to be restrained from sticking his hands into her abdomen to hold the bleeding vessels. No wonder the man was scarred by the events of that day. Anyone would be.

But it seemed that the person who was suffering most and who had had the least to do with it was Lucy, and that tore him apart.

CHAPTER SEVEN

EDITH had split her kneecap cleanly in two. It wasn't a starburst fracture, just a vertical break that needed to be held together so the strain put on it by bending her knee didn't pull the two sides apart. So it could have been worse, but nevertheless it was a very painful injury, and she'd be immobilised for some time.

And, as Lucy had thought, there was a possibility that she'd had a minor stroke.

Ben watched as Edith was wheeled away for her CT scan. The orthopaedic team would sort her knee out, and it was over to them now to play their part in her recovery. His job was done, and he phoned Lucy and told her what had happened.

'Oh, dear,' she said sadly. 'I hope it doesn't mean she can't cope on her own. I do so want her to be able to get back to her bungalow. She's lived there all her married life, since she and her husband bought it in 1967 when it was first built. He died earlier in the year, and she's lost without him. She'll be devastated if she has to move.'

'Poor woman, she's got enough on her plate. She was worried about her cat, by the way.'

'Dealt with. Her neighbour's looking after it for now. I expect she'll be in to see her soon. Ben, I'm glad you've phoned,

Kate's had another word with me about this meeting. She said the trust architect can make Thursday at four. Any chance you could do that?'

And no doubt Nick would be there this time. 'Yes, that'll be fine,' he agreed. He'd worry about Nick as and when he had to. 'What do you want for supper?'

'On Thursday?'

'Tonight,' he said, smiling. 'How about chicken?'

'Just had a chicken sandwich and an apple turnover. I ought to have something light and less full of fat. I'm going to be a barrel otherwise.'

'I've got news for you,' he said with a chuckle. 'Leave it to me, I'll sort it. I'll see you later. Are you staying the night at mine?'

'No,' she said, a little trace of regret in her voice. 'I should be at home.'

It didn't matter. She needed her rest, and there'd be plenty of time for them to be together in the future. 'OK. I'll see you later. Take care.'

He put the phone down and went back to work, whistling softly under his breath. Jo, his registrar, gave him an old-fashioned look. 'You look happy,' she said, almost accusingly, and he gave a slightly embarrassed laugh.

'There's no law against it, is there? And life's good.'

Or it would be if Nick Tremayne could only move on. One thing was for sure—Thursday was going to be interesting.

'So who's going to be here for this meeting this afternoon?' Nick asked.

'The trust architect, someone from the finance department, you, Marco, Lucy, Dragan and Ben Carter,' Kate said.

'Him again!'

Oh, here we go, Lucy thought, closing her eyes and letting her father and Kate Althorp argue it out.

'Why is it that everything that's mine, everything I hold dear, that man has to interfere with?'

If you only knew the half of it, Lucy thought, and opened her eyes to find Marco and Dragan both watching her thoughtfully. Oh, damn. Double damn, in fact. And then Kate looked at her, concern in her eyes, and she thought, Make that triple damn. With a cherry on top.

'I've got to get back to work,' she said, hoisting herself out of her chair and heading for the staffroom door, losing her mug on the draining-board on the way.

She shut herself in her consulting room for a moment, gathering her composure around her like a cloak. This afternoon's meeting was going to be a doozy, she thought, and she was dreading it.

She got through her morning surgery, went out on her visits, grabbed a sandwich, courtesy of Doris Trefussis, and declined the apple turnover in favour of a Cornish fairing brought in by Hazel Furse, the dumpy little head receptionist, who, as well as baking the best biscuits in the county, knew nearly as many people as Doris and ruled the appointments book with a will of iron.

Luckily she was also blessed with a great deal of common sense and, unlike a lot of receptionists Lucy had heard about, she didn't see her role as protecting the doctors from nagging patients who ought to wait their turn. So when Hazel popped in and said that a farmer, old Charlie Tew, was in Reception and urgently needed an appointment and could Lucy fit him in, she didn't hesitate.

She didn't have a surgery at the time, and was just about to see Chloe MacKinnon, the midwife, for an antenatal check, but something in Hazel's voice alerted her.

She went out into Reception and found him sitting there looking uncomfortable but not so bad that he would ring alarm bells. Not unless you took a really close look. She took him through to her consulting room and sat him down, her eyes making a quick inventory. Pale skin, clammy, sweating. 'What's the problem, Mr Tew?' she asked. 'You don't look very comfortable.'

'I pulled something,' he said bluntly. 'Heifer got stuck in the ditch and I couldn't get the tractor close enough, so we pulled 'er out with ropes. And I got this pain, Doc—right 'ere.' He pointed to the centre of his abdomen. 'It's like backache, only…'

He might have got a hernia. That was the most likely thing, or a ruptured psoas muscle, although that would tend to be at the side. The rectus abdominus muscle? Or…?

'Could you just slip your trousers down for me and pop onto the couch?' she asked, and he shuffled out of them and lay down cautiously, exposing a large, hairy abdomen encased in the biggest underpants she'd ever seen. She eased them down and pressed gently, then went very still.

Damn. She was right. The skin of his lower abdomen and legs was pale and mottled, and in the centre of his abdomen was a large, pulsating mass, beating in time with his heart. An abdominal aortic aneurism, she was sure, and if it was, there was no time to mess around. Left for very long, it would rupture. If it hadn't already, the blood enclosed in the space behind the peritoneum.

'I'm afraid you're going to have to go to hospital and have

an operation, Mr Tew,' she said gently. 'Stay there. I don't want you to get up, you just relax and keep still while I call an ambulance to take you to St Piran.'

'What, now? Only I've got a lot to do today. This heifer's put me right back. I could go in drekly, Doc.'

She smiled, knowing that the Cornish version of 'directly' was nothing of the sort.

'No, I think you need it a little sooner than directly,' she told him with a reassuring pat to his shoulder.

'Hernia, is it?'

'I don't think so. I think you might have a bulge in the wall of one of your blood vessels. And if you have, you'll need an operation now.' If you even get there, she added mentally. 'I'll call them straight away. Is there anyone with you?'

'No, I drove myself.'

She winced inwardly, knowing that if he'd had a collision and hit the steering-wheel or seat belt it would have been enough to finish him off.

'Stay there,' she warned again. Covering him with a blanket, she went out to Reception. 'Can you call an ambulance, Hazel, please? Mr Tew's got an aortic aneurism, I think. Urgent transfer—blue lights and all that. Cheers. I'll call the hospital and warn them. Oh, and could you ask Marco or Dragan if they're free to pop in? I know my father's got an antenatal class going.'

'Sure. Oh, there's your father now.'

'Thanks. Dad, old Mr Tew's here.' She filled him in quickly, then added, 'He's your patient. Do you want to examine him?'

He shook his head. 'No. I trust your judgement, Lucy, and if you're right he doesn't need any more poking about. I'll call the ambulance—fill them in. Hello, Mr Tew,' he said, sticking his head round the door. 'Gather you've been over-doing it. I'll see you in a minute, just going to call you some transport. Lucy, you might want to get a line in,' he added softly. 'Large-bore cannula. Two, if you can. And give him oxygen.'

'I was just about to. Thanks. Right, Mr Tew, I'm going to give you a little oxygen for now, and I'm just going to put a little needle in your arm, all ready for the hospital. It'll save time later.' She slipped it in easily, grateful for her time in A and E, then repeated the procedure in the other hand. 'There—one to let things in, one to let things out,' she said with a grin. 'Now, how about your wife? I think I'd better give her a call—can she get to the hospital?'

He frowned and studied her closely, as if the seriousness of it was suddenly dawning on him. 'How bad is it, Doc?' he asked. 'Is it going to finish me off?'

'I hope not,' she said honestly, not wanting to worry him but owing him the truth. 'But it is a major operation, and I think if I was your wife I'd finish you off anyway if you didn't let me know.'

His weather-beaten old face twisted into what could have been a smile, and he gave a dry chuckle. 'Well, we don't want that, do we, my bird? Best give her a call, then.'

Hazel came bustling in with a little tap on the door. 'Now, Charlie, I've phoned Grace and she's going straight to the hospital,' she told him, getting there ahead of them. 'The boy's going to take her, and she'll have some pyjamas for you and your wash things.'

'Good idea,' he said, and Lucy wondered if he really had the slightest clue how much danger he was in, and hoped, most sincerely, that he didn't. There was a difference between knowing that something was serious and realising it could kill you at any second.

She saw the flashing lights coming down Harbour Road, and for the second time that week Maggie Pascoe came to the rescue.

'Taxi!' she said with a bright smile, leaving her partner Mike to wheel the trolley in and going over to Mr Tew to pat his hand. 'Hello, Charlie, my love. What's this I hear about you pulling heifers out of ditches, you silly old goat? You should be leaving that to the young 'uns and issuing instructions on the sidelines. Should have thought that was right up your street.'

Charlie chuckled, and Lucy realised they must know each other well. Not that that surprised her. Nearly everyone knew everyone, and if they didn't, they knew someone who did.

'I s'pose you're old enough to have your driver's licence,' Charlie said drily, and Maggie rolled her eyes.

'Oh, no, I just stole the ambulance for a bit of fun—felt like a joy-ride. Anyway, I don't have to drive it, I get to sit in the back and tell you off all the way to the hospital. Right, you stay there, my love, we'll slide you across. Lucy, let go of that, you aren't pulling anything!' she said, and Lucy let go of the sheet and watched as Maggie and Mike pulled him easily, sheet and all, across the Pat-slide and onto the trolley.

In moments he was tucked up in a blanket, strapped down and away, and again Lucy rang Ben and warned him. 'I'm sending you a patient with a query abdominal aortic aneurism. No known history, but he's not the complaining sort so he may have had a bit of a bulge for ages. Whatever, it's a large midline pulsatile mass, and I don't like the look of him at all. I don't know if you'll still be there or if you'll be on your way here, but he needs to go straight to Theatre.'

'Are you certain?'

'As I can be.'

'That's good enough for me,' he said. 'I'll tell them to expect him and get a theatre slot primed. And I'll see you in an hour for this wretched meeting. Should I wear my stab vest?'

She laughed a little uneasily. 'I'm sure that won't be necessary. It'll be highly civilised. I'll make sure we've got plenty of Hazel's Cornish fairings to keep us going. We can always throw them at each other if it hots up.'

'Oh, no, that would be such a waste. I've heard about those biscuits of hers, even from this distance. She feeds them to the paramedics, apparently.'

'Well, don't get too excited. If Dad's found them, there may not be any left.'

He chuckled, said goodbye and hung up, and she buzzed through to Chloe. 'I'm sorry, I got held up with a patient. Do you want me today or not?'

'Yes, when you're ready. I've just seen my last patient, so come on up. Don't forget your urine sample.'

'As if,' she mocked, and went via the loo. 'Here—hot off the press,' she said, handing it over.

Chloe tested it and nodded. 'It's fine. Good. And your blood pressure's nice and low. I haven't seen you for days, though. I get the feeling you're doing too much. How are you feeling generally?'

Tired? Stressed? Worried sick that her father and her lover were about to kill each other in less than an hour? 'I'm fine, too,' she said, but her smile couldn't have been convincing, because Chloe gave a sceptical grunt.

'You look exhausted. You must be overdoing it. Maybe you should stop work sooner.'

'I can't—' she began, but Chloe just tutted and pointed at the scales.

'You haven't gained anything. That's the second week in a row. I think you should have another scan. They were a bit worried about your placenta with the last one, weren't they? Thought it was a bit low down?'

'Not very low. They were talking about another scan at thirty-four weeks to check it, but they were pretty sure I wouldn't need a C-section.'

'And what are you? Thirty-two weeks on Saturday? I think you should have it now.'

She sighed, then thought of Ben and how much he'd like to be there. 'OK,' she agreed. 'I'll give them a call.'

'No, *I'll* give them a call—make sure it happens. You take care of that little one, Lucy.'

'I will.'

'I'll book you in for the scan tomorrow morning.'

'Tomorrow!'

'Yes. Tomorrow—morning. Get Hazel to reschedule your patients. And get Ben to feed you over the weekend.'

She looked up, startled, into Chloe's wide and seemingly innocent green eyes. 'Why should Ben feed me?'

'Oh, Lucy, come on. You've been seen together. People talk. All my patients are commenting this morning—Dr Lucy's boyfriend is gorgeous, isn't he? Have you seen him? Beautiful car. Do you think Dr Lucy and her lovely Mr Carter will get married before the baby's born?'

'What? That's crazy!'

'They saw you at the barbeque, Lucy. Nobody's seen you with anyone since, and they certainly didn't before. You don't date any more than I do. And you've been seen with him again recently. And they all know that he's bought Tregorran House. It's gone through the village like wildfire, and it's obvious to everyone but your father why he's done it.'

She stared into Chloe's gentle, caring eyes another second, then looked away hastily, her eyes prickling with tears. 'I hadn't realised gossip was that rife.'

'Oh, Lucy, this is Penhally. And it's only because everybody loves you and wants a happy ending for you.'

She swallowed hard. 'I wish.'

Chloe squeezed her arm. 'Come on. You'll get there. Fancy coming round to mine this evening and letting me feed you?'

She opened her mouth, shut it, then said, 'I ought to talk to Ben. My father doesn't know yet but, judging by the sound of it, it won't be long.'

'OK. But make him feed you properly, and get an early night. And go straight to the hospital tomorrow—in fact, sit there, I'll book you in now.'

She rang the hospital while Lucy sat obediently, and thought about her friend's revelations. Did the whole world *really* know about Ben? Or did it just seem like it?

'Right. Eight-thirty. So you can stay at Ben's, and you won't have such a long drive in the morning.'

'I can organise my own life,' she grumbled gently, but Chloe just laughed and opened the door for her.

'Of course you can. I'll get them to call me with the results. Don't forget to eat.'

'Stop nagging,' Lucy said, and went into the staffroom. It

was empty, but the coffee-tables had been moved to the centre, the chairs were grouped around them and there were clean mugs set out on the side next to a tin of Hazel's fairings.

Eat, Chloe had said, so she ate. She had one, then another, and then there was a tap on the door and Ben came in.

'Hi!' she said, overjoyed to see him, and he shut the door and pulled her into his arms.

'How's my favourite girl today?' he murmured, smiling down at her and nuzzling her nose with his.

She sighed and rested her head on his chest. 'In trouble. I've just had a lecture from my midwife. Apparently I need to eat more.'

'Well, I keep telling you that. Are there any of Hazel's biscuits around?'

'Yes, in that tin—and I've had two, before you start. And I've got to have a scan tomorrow morning—eight-thirty. Can I stay with you tonight?'

He paused, his hands on the tin, and turned back to her. 'Of course you can.'

'Do you want—?'

'Can I—?'

They spoke together, and Ben laughed and said, 'You first.'

'I was going to ask if you want to come.'

'And I was going to ask if I could.'

'That's a yes, then.'

'If you don't mind.'

'I'd love you to be there.'

He tipped his head on one side and studied her thoughtfully. 'Funny time for a scan.'

'My placenta was a little low at the eighteen-week scan, so they wanted to check at thirty-four.'

His brows clamped together. 'Low? How low?'

'Nothing to worry about. It's just a routine check.'

'But you're not even quite thirty-two weeks,' he said, holding her at arm's length and searching her eyes. 'So why now? Two weeks early? Is this because you're not gaining enough? It's that bad?'

She sighed and confessed. 'I haven't put any weight on for two weeks.'

'Then I'm definitely going to be there,' he said firmly. 'Now, about these fairings,' he said, opening the tin and holding one out to her.

'Ben, I've had two.'

'That's not enough. Come on, open wide.'

She was laughing up at him, pushing him away and fighting over the biscuit when the door opened and her father walked in and stopped dead in the doorway.

Oh, rats. Of all the timing…

Ben dropped his hands, stepped away from her and met his ice-cold eyes. 'Dr Tremayne.'

'Carter,' he said, but she could tell the word nearly choked him. Even the sound of Ben's name had been like a curse for years. He hated him. Blamed him for her mother's death, and hated him, and no amount of reasoning would get him to see sense.

This afternoon, clearly, wasn't going to be the time. His taut, still firm jaw was clenched, the dark eyes unyielding as he stared at Ben for an endless, breathless moment.

Please, don't let him be rude, Lucy prayed. Don't let him start anything. Not here, not with everyone due here in moments.

God was obviously otherwise engaged.

'Bit early, aren't you?' Nick said softly, but there was a deadly edge to his voice that made Lucy's heart beat faster.

Ben shrugged. 'Not really. I didn't want to be late. I consider this expansion to be very important for the local community, and since I'm part of it I take my contribution very seriously—'

Her father's snort cut him off and his mouth tightened. 'Really? I can see just how seriously you were taking it.'

'Dad!' she cut in, trying to avert a scene. 'Come on. This isn't the time or the place.'

His eyes flicked back to her. 'No—and I would have thought you could have found yourself something more useful to do than fighting over the biscuits,' he growled, and she felt her temper start to fray.

'Actually, he was trying to get me to look after myself,' she pointed out, but her father just snorted again.

'It'll be a cold day in hell when a member of the Tremayne family needs advice on their health from Ben Carter,' he said, his voice harsh. 'And I would have thought you'd have greater loyalty to your mother than to be playing the fool with the man who—'

'Leave my mother out of this,' she snapped. 'You know perfectly well that Ben wasn't at fault.'

'Do I?' He looked Ben up and down with eyes that blazed with anger and pain, and a lesser man would have flinched.

Ben just calmly returned his stare. 'Dr Tremayne, this was settled two years ago—'

'You expect me to believe that report? You know damn well the inquiry was rigged.'

Lucy gasped, and there was a muted sound of reproach from Kate. Behind him, she could see the practice manager with the trust architect and finance executive in tow, the other GPs clustered on the landing behind them.

How much had they all heard? She didn't know. Anything would be too much. A muscle twitched in Ben's jaw, but apart from that and the dull run of colour on his cheekbones there was no other reaction from him.

'I'll pretend I didn't hear that,' he said, and made to turn away, but Nick's voice stopped him in his tracks.

'What—the truth?' her father went on doggedly, but Ben had had enough.

He turned back, eyes blazing with anger, and said, his voice deathly quiet, 'Dr Tremayne, I'm not here because I want to be, but because I believe in this project. I was asked to contribute, and if you don't want me here, all you have to do is say the word and I'll leave. Believe me, I have plenty to do.'

They glared at each other, then Nick took a deep breath and let it out. 'We're in the same boat, then. I'm only here because I want what's best for my practice and my community. You, I keep being told, are the best. So stay, and we'll get this damned meeting over, and then we can all go and get on with our lives. But stay away from my daughter, Carter. There are some nasty rumours flying around, and I hope they're just that. If I ever hear you've laid so much as a finger on her—'

'You'll what?' Lucy cut in, furious with him and on the verge of tears. 'He's a friend of mine. I can't help it if you don't like that, but I'm twenty-nine, for heaven's sake! You don't get to dictate my friendships, so just get over it and let's move on. Everybody's waiting.'

Kate gave Nick a none-too-gentle shove in the ribs, and

he took a step forward. Ben moved back out of his way and the cameo broke up, everyone busily settling themselves down and not knowing quite where to look.

Except Ben. He sat opposite her while Kate made the tea and handed it round, his eyes fixed on her, and every time she looked up he was there, the look in his eyes reassuring.

'Right, shall I introduce everybody?' Kate said, and gradually the awkward silence eased. She and Ben both put in their contributions on the proposed plans, she talked the architect through it on paper, Dragan and Marco chipped in with their take on it—only Nick was silent, speaking when he was spoken to but otherwise just watching, his eyes never leaving Ben's face.

He knows, she thought with sudden certainty. Or thinks he does. He certainly suspects.

'What do you think, Lucy?'

Think? Think about what? She dragged her mind back to the discussion, apologised and asked Marco to repeat what he'd said.

'We were talking about the advisability of delaying the implementation of the new MIU until after you return from maternity leave,' Kate said.

'Um—no,' she said, wondering if she would be returning from maternity leave or if she'd even have a job to come back to once her father knew the truth. 'I think you should go ahead, at least with the planning stage. That'll take some time, won't it?'

'Indeed,' the architect said. 'I need to examine the outside of the building before it's dark, and see where you're proposing to put this extension.'

'Right behind you, down there,' Kate said, getting up and

pointing through the window. 'Dragan, would you like to show him? To save Lucy going down?'

'I can do it,' she said, and got to her feet at the same time as Ben and her father. 'No, really, I can do it. Ben—your comments might be useful,' she said, and they trooped out, leaving Kate and the other members of the practice to discuss financing it with the bean counter, while her father glowered after them in brooding silence.

'You OK?' Ben asked softly, and she nodded.

'This would be the link through if we went two-storey,' she pointed out to the architect as they stood on the landing. 'At the moment it's staff cloakroom and showering facilities, but there's a big lobby area that could be taken to make a way through.'

She showed him around, then they went downstairs and out into the garden.

'Hmm.' The architect was studying the land behind, the steep granite escarpment behind the practice which ended in an outcrop of rock right where they wanted to build. 'You want to put it here?'

'It's dead space, and it links in well,' she explained.

The architect frowned. 'I don't know. I think it could be very expensive. The rock would have to be cut away and there isn't room round the side to bring in heavy gear to do it. Is there anywhere else? At the front, for instance?'

She struggled to pay attention. 'Not really. We need all the car parking space we can get our hands on, so we can't take that, and there isn't enough room at the side.'

'Pity.' The architect looked up at the building to the side of them. 'What's this?'

'A boatyard—repairs, engineering works and sail loft, and

a chandlery. Don't worry, we've already considered it. The practice manager is co-owner, but there isn't any possibility of taking part of the land, even if we could afford to buy it from them. They're already overcrowded.'

'Hmm. How about going out over the top of the car parking area?' he suggested as they walked back round to the front. 'It would be expensive, but not as expensive as buying the land next door or shifting the rock. Planning might be a bit of an issue. I'll have to think about that one and come back to you on it.'

He glanced at his watch. 'Right, I need to get a move on. Let's go and break the news to the others, and we'll have to reconvene after I've had a think. Can I borrow your plans? I'll get them copied and have them sent back to you tomorrow.'

'Of course,' she agreed, and they went back upstairs.

'Ah, you're back. More tea?' Kate offered, but the two men from the trust shook their heads.

'We need to get away. If we could just take these?'

They were folding the plans, shuffling paper into brief-cases, putting on their coats, and Lucy sneaked a quick glance at her father. He was talking to Kate and the finance man, ignoring Ben, and as she looked away she caught Dragan's eye.

He raised an enquiring brow, and she smiled reassuringly. He nodded, apparently satisfied, and, glancing at his watch, he stood up. 'If you'll all excuse me, I have a visit to make.'

'Really?' she said as he walked past her. 'I didn't think you were on call this evening.'

He smiled a little awkwardly. 'I'm not, but there's a certain dog who seems to be expecting me to go and play games with her. And I may well be offered supper, so I don't have to cook. As I have no food, that would be good.'

'Ah.' She smiled. 'Well, give Melinda my love,' she said, and watched in fascination as his neck darkened slightly. Poor Dragan, it was mean to tease him. He was such a serious, thoughtful man so much of the time, and on the few occasions she'd seen him with Melinda he'd looked genuinely happy.

'I will,' he said, then paused and looked at Ben, standing beside her. 'Look after her, OK? She's looking tired. She's doing too much.'

No! Don't tell Ben to look after me in front of my father, she thought frantically, but Nick was busy talking and Ben just smiled.

'Leave her to me,' he said softly. 'I'll take care of her.'

'Good. Someone needs to.' And he nodded to the others and left. The men from the trust followed, then Marco and, rather than have to talk any more to her father, she propelled Ben towards the door, grabbing his coat on the way.

'In a hurry to get rid of me?' he murmured as they went downstairs.

'Not at all. I'm in a hurry to get you away from my father before you kill each other. Ben, I think he knows.'

He stopped dead on the bottom stair. 'Really?'

'Really. Come on. We'll talk about it this evening. I've got a surgery starting in a minute.'

'I've rescheduled you,' Hazel said, overhearing. 'Chloe told me to, so I've put your patients in with your father and Marco, and you've got tomorrow off.'

She opened her mouth to argue, then changed her mind. She felt sorry for Marco, but her father deserved it. She smiled at Hazel. 'Thank you.'

'Pleasure. Oh, and Charlie's wife called. He's out of

Theatre and he's in ITU. Apparently they got him there just in time, so well done.'

'Good,' she said, then added more softly, 'At least that's one thing I've done right today.'

'You've done nothing wrong today,' Ben said gruffly.

'My father wouldn't agree. I'm so angry with him.'

'Don't be. He's just hurting.'

'Ben, it's slander!'

He just smiled wryly and gave her a slow, lazy wink. 'Relax. I'll see you soon at my place. I'll go via the supermarket and get you something jumping with vitamins and calories.'

She let her smile out at last. 'You're a star,' she said softly. 'I'll see you later.'

He went out, crossing the car park briskly and getting into his car just as her father came up beside her. 'I want to talk to you,' he said firmly, and taking her elbow he propelled her into her consulting room and shut the door.

'About Carter,' he began, but she was watching Ben through the window, turning the car and lifting his hand in farewell, and she thought of the dignity with which he'd handled the whole awful, embarrassing situation and she wanted to kill her father.

She turned back to him, her whole body trembling with reaction, and shook her head. 'You had no right to say those things to him. No right at all! It's just lies, and you're flinging them around willy-nilly in front of everybody. It would serve you right if he took you to court, and it's just rubbish, Dad! You know why she died.'

'And so do you—and if you're blinded by his lies, then you're not the daughter your mother and I thought you were. There are some ugly rumours flying around, Lucy. I don't want to believe what I'm hearing, and I don't. Just don't give me any reason to doubt you, because the last thing I want to hear is that that bastard has fathered my grandchild.'

She stared at him, her eyes filling with tears, and then looked across the car park. Ben had pulled out into Harbour Road, but she could follow him—

'Lucy! Lucy, come back here.'

'No,' she said, turning back to look her father in the eye. 'No, this time you've gone too far. The only bastard in all of this is you—oh, and your grandchild, and I'm just about to do something about that.'

She scooped up her bag, ran upstairs for her coat and then ran down, fighting back the tears. Her father was still standing in the door of her consulting room, his jaw set, and without sparing him a second glance she went out to her car, got in it and drove off after Ben.

CHAPTER EIGHT

BEN was gutted.

Gutted for Lucy, and furious with her father. If Lucy didn't manage to silence him soon, then he was going to, because this couldn't be allowed to go on. Tremayne could think what the hell he liked about him, but he wasn't going to go spreading it around the county like that. How he hadn't hit him he had no idea.

He called the solicitor on the way to the supermarket, not really expecting him to be at work still, but to his surprise Simon answered.

'Hi. You're working late. It's Ben Carter—I just wondered if there was any news.'

'Oh, hi, Ben. It's all done,' Simon said, to his surprise. 'Actually, I was just going to call you on my way out of the office. I've had confirmation in writing that the purchaser's quite happy for you to continue to live in your present house and rent it from him until the end of February, if necessary, so as you instructed I've gone ahead and completed on both houses today. The Orchard Way house is sold, and Tregorran House is yours. Congratulations. The paperwork's all in the post, and the keys of Tregorran House are with the agent.'

'Amazing,' he said, stunned. 'God, you're efficient! Thank you, Simon. You're a star.'

'My pleasure. If there's anything else I can do, just ask.'

Like getting a restraining order on Nick Tremayne? 'I'll bear it in mind,' he said, biting his tongue, and cut the connection, his mind whirling.

Hell's teeth, he'd done it. He'd got Lucy's house.

He threw back his head and laughed in relief. There'd been a few moments in the past week when he'd wondered if Nick would try and block the sale, or at least throw up something he could to stall it, but apparently not. He was evidently as pleased to get rid of it as Ben was to have acquired it.

Now all he had to do was tell Lucy. He couldn't wait to see her face.

He wasn't there.

Of course he wasn't. He was going via the supermarket, and he might be ages. And she should have gone via her house and picked up some things, if she was staying here tonight.

She shut her eyes, dropped her head back against the headrest and sighed. She'd got herself so psyched up, convinced herself she'd be able to do this, but now he wasn't here, she was losing her nerve. What if he—?

Stop it, she told herself. Deal with it later.

For now she'd ring him, get him to pick her up some knickers and deodorant at the shop. She fished in her bag for her phone and called him.

'Could you buy me some knickers for tomorrow?' she asked, and he gave a strangled laugh.

'What kind? Not those tiny scraps of string.'

She couldn't help the smile. He loved the tiny scraps of string. 'No, something a bit more—'

'Stop there. Just a bit more will do.'

'Not granny knickers,' she pleaded, but he just laughed.

'Don't panic. What else?'

She gave him a list, and he grunted. 'Right. I was about done. Give me ten minutes and I'll be on my way.'

She shut her eyes and leaned back and waited, trying to be calm, trying not to think negatively, and finally she saw the sweep of his headlights against her closed lids, and heard his car pull up beside hers and stop.

Then her door opened, and Ben reached in and hugged her. 'Come on, out you get, we're celebrating.'

'Celebrating?' she said, wondering what on earth they had to celebrate when her father had been so unreasonable—unless, of course, he'd turned into a mind reader—but he was grinning from ear to ear and taking off her seat belt, all but hauling her out. 'Celebrating what?' she asked as he scooped up the carrier bags from the passenger seat and shoved his car door shut with his knee.

'Aha! Come inside.'

'Celebrating what?' she repeated, trailing him in, and he put the shopping down, picked her up in his arms and whirled her round, laughing.

'The house—it's ours. We've got it—completed.' He put her down very gently on her feet, cradled her face in his hands and kissed her tenderly. 'You've got your house, my darling. As of today we are the official owners of Tregorran House. We can get the keys tomorrow.'

She was confused. 'But—what about this house? Didn't you have to sell it first—move out of it?'

'Not yet. The new owner's renting it to me until the end of February, to give us time to sort the other one out before we move in.' He stopped talking and searched her face, his eyes concerned. 'You will move in with me, won't you? Live with me? In the house? Even if we have separate rooms—'

'No.' She put her fingers on his lips. 'Not separate rooms. I want us together, in the room my grandparents had. When I was little and the cockerel woke me, I used to get into bed with Grannie in the morning and snuggle up, and it was lovely. I've always loved that room.'

She felt her eyes fill, and blinked the tears away so she could see his dear, wonderful face. 'Oh, Ben, thank you,' she said, and then the tears won and she closed her eyes and let them slip down her cheeks.

'Hey, you aren't supposed to cry,' he said softly, and she laughed and hugged him, bubbling over with joy.

'Sorry. Just happy. Ignore me.'

'No. I'm going to make you a cup of tea, and sit you down with your feet up, and then I'm going to cook you supper.'

'I want vegetables.'

'You're getting vegetables. Roasted root vegetables, steamed cauliflower and broccoli, and roast lamb.'

'Roast lamb?'

'Don't you like it?'

'I love it,' she admitted. 'I just never cook it for myself. I don't think I've had roast lamb since Mum died—' She broke off, the emotions of the day suddenly overwhelming her, and Ben muttered something under his breath, wrapped her in his arms and cradled her against his heart.

'Oh, sweetheart, I'm so sorry.'

'What for?' she asked, choked.

'That you haven't got your mother now,' he said, going right to the heart of it. 'She ought to be here for you when you're having your first baby, and I'm so sad for you that she can't be.'

'She'll never see my children,' she said, finally voicing one of the huge regrets that had plagued her since her mother's death. She gave a hiccuping sob, and he held her tighter, rubbing her back gently and cuddling her while she wept. 'Oh, sorry, I'm being so silly,' she said, scrubbing the tears away with the palms of her hands.

'No, you're not. You're sad, and you're tired, and you've had another fight with your father.'

'Oh, I know. He's a nightmare. I don't know what to do with him. I want to tell him about the baby—I'm desperate to talk to him, for him to come to terms with you being its father, but I just don't see it happening. He's so awful to you—it's just not like him, and it's as if I've lost him, too.'

'He's just angry that she died, and a little lost without her, I guess. He needs someone to lash out at, and I'm convenient. I can cope with it, Lucy.'

'But the things he was saying, about the inquiry—'

'Are just rubbish. I know that, he knows that—we all know that. Your mother died because of a whole series of events. She was as much to blame as anyone else. If she'd been a bit more forthright about her condition and told your father how ill she was, or if she'd come to us sooner, it would have been quite different. But she left it too late, and she didn't check in, and nobody spotted her. It was the whole chain of events that led to her death, and what caused it ultimately was the number of painkillers she'd taken.'

'And he feels guilty that he didn't spot anything, that she

could have been feeling that bad and he just didn't notice.'
She shook her head. 'If only I'd been at home at the time,
but I was away on a course the day she was taken really ill,
and I hadn't been home for ages. I was still living in the hospital after finishing my A and E rotation—it was only days
after I'd finished, if you remember. If only I'd still been
there, she would have asked for me, and I could have done
something…'

Her voice was tortured, and he wanted to weep for her.
There was nothing she could have done. Nothing anyone could
have done—including him. He hadn't caused Annabel's death.
He knew that. Deep down, he knew it, but there was still a sick
feeling inside him whenever he thought about the waste of her
life, and today's row with her husband had brought it all back
in spades. As it was, he just felt sick at heart and deeply sorry
for everything that had happened, even though it hadn't been
his fault.

He wondered if Lucy really believed that he wasn't to
blame or, if despite all her defence of him, somewhere deep
inside there was a bit of her that wasn't quite sure. And in any
case, her father still clearly blamed him for everything that
had gone so horribly wrong the day Annabel had died.

How were they ever going to sort it out if Nick wouldn't
even discuss it?

'You mustn't blame yourself,' he told her gently. 'There's
no way you were at fault. You weren't even there.'

'No. Nobody was. She gave so much of herself to us all,
and when she needed us, none of us were there for her. I think
she felt she didn't matter, that we were all too busy to be disturbed for something as trivial as her illness, and we must
have let her think that. Four doctors in the family, Ben, and

we didn't even realise she was sick. We're all to blame in that, and Dad's busy trying to lay the blame at someone else's door. I feel as if I've lost them both.'

She straightened up and gave him a wan smile that twisted his heart. 'Did you say something about tea?'

'I did,' he said, and gave her a gentle push towards the sofa. 'Go on, sit down, put your feet up and have a rest. I'll bring it through in a minute. I just want to put the supper in the oven. It won't take long, it's only a fillet.'

'Oh, gorgeous.' She gave him a weary smile. 'Thanks, Ben,' she said softly, and he swallowed the lump in his throat. 'Any time.'

He went into the kitchen, took his feelings for Nick out on the unsuspecting vegetables, shoved the meat in the oven once it was hot, poured the tea and took it through.

At first he thought she was asleep, but then he saw the tears trickling down her face, and he put the tea down with a sigh, sat next to her and pulled her gently into his arms. 'Oh, Lucy.'

It felt so good to let him hold her. She rested against him for a moment, then tilted her head back and looked searchingly into his eyes. All she could see was love and concern and a fathoms-deep kindness that went all the way to the bottom of his heart. She loved him so much, and if he loved her, too, as much as his eyes said he did, then maybe…

She gathered up her courage. 'Ben, when you found out about the baby two weeks ago, and we were talking about it, at my flat—you said some things.'

He groaned and closed his eyes. 'Oh, hell. I said all sorts of things, but if any of them are upsetting you, for God's sake tell me—'

'No. Not at all. I just wondered—you said we shouldn't

rule certain things out, and I wondered if you still felt that way. You see— Oh, I don't know how to say this, but I just feel… Ben, will you marry me?'

His eyes flew open. 'Marry?' He stared at her for an endless moment, and then his eyes filled and he looked away and gave a short cough of laughter. 'Oh, hell, now *I'm* going to cry,' he said, and dragged her further into his arms. 'Of course I'll marry you, you stupid woman. I'd love to marry you. Nothing would make me happier.'

His lips found hers, and he rained soft, desperate kisses all over her mouth, her jaw, her eyes, back to her lips, then with a last, lingering, tender kiss, he lifted his head. 'Of course I'll marry you,' he repeated. 'I'd be honoured.'

She smiled, a pretty watery event, she thought, but he was hardly going to be able to criticise her for that. She lifted her hand and gently smoothed the tears from his cheeks, then kissed him once more. 'You don't have to go that far,' she said a little unsteadily, 'but I'm so glad you said yes, because if you'd said no…'

'Not a chance,' he said, his laugh ragged and cut off short. His arm tightened around her, and he tucked her in against his side and leant forward, passing her her tea then going back for his. 'When did you have in mind? Soon, I would think?'

She shrugged diffidently, still trying to absorb the fact that it was really going to happen. 'Before the baby comes?'

'And what about your father?'

'Oh, lord.' She sighed, considering the ramifications. 'What about my father? I'll ask him. I'll have to, and if I'm honest, I'd love to have him there, but I don't know if he'll come, and I really don't think it matters any more. It's not him I'm marrying, it's you, and I'm not going to let him spoil it.'

'Good. And I'll do everything I can to make you happy. You know that.'

'You already do, Ben.' She rested her head against his chest, sipped her tea and sighed. 'We ought to celebrate with champagne,' she said, 'what with getting the house and getting married, but I probably shouldn't drink.'

'No, and I don't need to. I've got all I need right here.'

'What, a cup of tea?' she teased, and he chuckled and hugged her.

'Absolutely. So, tomorrow, after your scan, I think we should go and get a ring, and then sort out a venue. Register office or church?'

She thought of the pretty little church up on the headland, next to the coastguard lookout station and the lighthouse— the church where her mother, grandfather and uncle were all buried. It would seem so right…

'The church—St Mark's, in Penhally Bay, up on the headland,' she told him. 'If we can. I don't know. I'm not sure of the rules.'

'We'll find out. And if we can't do that, maybe we can be married in the register office and have a blessing in the church later.'

'Mmm. Ben?'

'Mmm?'

'I hate to be practical, but is the supper OK?'

He jackknifed to his feet and ran to the kitchen, yanking down the oven door and letting out a cloud of smoke and steam.

'It's OK,' he yelled. 'Just.'

She got slowly to her feet and went through, to find him examining the vegetables. One or two were a little singed around the edges, but the rest were fine and the meat looked perfect.

'Gosh, it smells fantastic. I'm really hungry. What about the cauliflower and broccoli?'

'Two minutes, while I make the gravy. Sit.'

'Yes, sir,' she said, but she sat anyway and watched him while he dished up, and then she ate everything he put on her plate.

'More?'

She laughed and shook her head. 'No, I'm full. No room now with the bump in the way, but Chloe would be proud of you for getting so many calories into me.'

'I'll give you ice cream later,' he said, and shooed her back into the sitting room while he cleared up.

She went quite willingly. Chloe's news about her weight had worried her, and she realised she probably had been over-doing things. Well, not any more. She needed to give her baby the best possible chance, and if that meant Ben loading the dishwasher alone, so be it.

So she sat, and switched on the television, and after a while Ben came and joined her, and when her eyes started to droop, he carried her up to bed, snuggled her spoon-like against his chest and fell asleep with his hand curved protectively over the baby and the reassuring beat of his heart against her back...

'There—everything looks fine. There's not an awful lot of fluid—maybe you need to drink more. But the position of the placenta isn't a worry, it's moved up enough that it's away from the cervix.'

Ben stared, transfixed, at the screen. He could hear Jan

Warren, the obstetrician, talking, but all he could see was his baby, arms and legs waving, heart beating nice and steadily.

'Would you like to know what sex it is?'

'No,' they said in unison, and he laughed awkwardly. 'Well, it's not really my call.'

'I don't care, so long as everything's all right,' Lucy said.

'Well, it all looks absolutely fine. The baby's a good size, everything seems perfectly normal—there, how about that for a photo?'

Jan clicked a button, and seconds later handed them a grainy, black and white image of their child. Ben felt his eyes prickle and blinked hard, and Lucy handed it to him. 'Here— put it in your wallet,' she said, and he nodded, but he didn't put it away.

Not yet. He wanted to look at it a little longer, while Lucy— in respectable knickers!—was wiped clean of the ultrasound gel and helped up to her feet.

'I need a pee,' she said bluntly, and the obstetrician smiled.

'Go on, then. I'll see you in a couple of weeks.'

'Fine,' she said, and all but ran out of the door. Jan gave Ben a searching look as he gave the photo one last lingering stare and put it away.

'Can I take it you have a vested interest in this baby, Ben?' she asked, and he laughed softly.

'I don't think it's going to be a secret for long,' he admitted. 'We're getting married as soon as we can.'

Her face broke into a smile. 'Well, congratulations.'

'Thanks. Is the baby really OK? She's not been looking after herself.'

'Babies are very good at doing that for themselves, unless the conditions are really unfavourable, and yours is fine.'

'Good. Thanks, Jan.' He felt his shoulders drop and, shaking her hand, he headed out into the corridor to wait for Lucy. She wasn't long, and he put his arm around her shoulders and hugged her. 'OK?'

'Fine. Relieved—in every sense of the word.'

He chuckled and they fell into step side by side.

'Where are we going next?' she asked.

'My office, to phone the vicar? How do you feel about coming down to A and E to see everyone and give them the news?'

'The news?' she said, looking up him and sounding puzzled. 'What news?'

'That we're getting married?'

'Oh! Yes, of course,' she agreed. 'I thought you meant that the baby was OK.'

'No. They don't know about it, or at least not from anything I've said, so if you'd rather not?'

She took a deep breath. 'No. No, I'd like them to know. I want everyone to know that you're the father. I'm proud of the fact, and I love you, and I've got nothing to hide. Anyway, it would be nice to see them again.'

And slipping her hand into his, she walked beside him into A and E. It was the first time she'd been there since her mother had died, and as they passed Resus, she looked in and paused.

'Oh, Lucy, I'm sorry,' he said, immediately picking up on her feelings, but she just smiled at him.

'Don't be. It's fine. It's just a room, and she's hardly the first or the last. And I know you did everything you possibly could.'

'Do you really believe that?' he asked quietly, and she looked up at him and saw doubt in his eyes.

'Oh, Ben, of course I believe it!' she exclaimed, resting a hand over his heart. 'I know you did everything. Don't for a moment tar me with the same brush as my father.'

'I don't.'

'Good.' She looked back at Resus and sighed. 'I just wish my father hadn't seen it.'

'No. That was awful. Nobody should see someone they love in those circumstances. It's hard enough when you're detached.'

'I know. I remember.' She dragged in a breath and smiled up at him. 'Shall we get this over, then? Tell them you're getting married and break the hearts of all the women in the department who fancy they're in love with you?'

'Idiot,' he said, laughing. Putting his arm around her shoulder, he led her away from Resus to the work desk in the central area.

'Ah, Jo,' he said, greeting a young woman who was bent over some notes. 'Jo, this is Lucy. Lucy, my registrar, Jo. Um, we've got some news,' he told her, and she looked at Lucy's bump pointedly and her eyes twinkled.

'You don't say,' she teased.

He chuckled. 'Actually, the news is I'd like you to cover for me for the rest of the day. I've got some arranging to do—we're getting married.'

'Oh, Ben, that's fabulous!' she said, throwing her arms round his neck and hugging him. 'Hey, guys! Guess what! Ben's getting married!'

They must have come out of the woodwork, Lucy thought, because in the next few seconds the place was swarming with people, many of whom remembered her, and she was hugged and kissed and the baby exclaimed over, and finally they got away into Ben's office and shut the door.

'Phew!' she said, and Ben laughed apologetically and hugged her.

'You OK?'

'I'm fine. They're lovely. Right, can we ring the vicar now?'

An hour later they were sitting in his office at the vicarage in Penhally, and to her relief Mr Kenner was being more than helpful.

'I'd be delighted to marry you both,' he said fervently, taking Lucy's hand and squeezing it. 'I've been worried about you. Ever since your mother died, there's been such an air of sadness about you and your father, and it's wonderful to see you so happy. And I imagine you want to move this on quite swiftly?'

She laughed at the irony. 'I think that would be good. I know it sounds old-fashioned, but I really want my baby— *our* baby—to be born in wedlock. Do they still use that dreadful expression?'

He chuckled and let go of her hand. 'I think you've summed it up very well—and some things are meant to be old-fashioned,' he added, unwittingly echoing her own thoughts. 'Ben, I take it you're quite happy with this marriage?'

'More than happy,' he said, and any doubt she'd had vanished into thin air at the conviction in his voice. His arm slid around her shoulders and squeezed, and she leant against him with a smile.

'Excellent. Right, the procedure is this. The banns have to be read out in church on three consecutive Sundays before the wedding—so as it's a Friday, if we start this weekend, you should be able to get married in just over a fortnight. So two weeks on Monday would be the earliest, in law.'

'Can we do it then?'

He hesitated, then smiled. 'Of course. It's usually my day off, but under the circumstances, and since I can't think of a single thing I'd rather be doing than joining you two in marriage, I'd be delighted to do it then. Do you have a time in mind?'

'No. Well—I don't know who's going to be there. Um—can we make it twelve? Ben, what do you think? Then people from the practice can be there, and we can go to the Smugglers' for lunch perhaps.'

He met her eyes. People from the practice? She could see him thinking it, wondering if her father would come. And in truth she had no idea, but she had to ask him.

'I think if twelve would be all right with Mr Kenner, it would be fine.' His eyes flicked back to the vicar, and he nodded.

'Twelve it is, then. Right, we have some paperwork to attend to next.'

So that was it. They were getting married, and once the banns were read out on Sunday, the whole village would know.

She had to see her father, but not now. Not in the middle of surgery, or while he was trying to get out on his visits, or when he had a clinic. And they had something else to do first, something she'd much rather do, and she couldn't wait another minute...

'You know, with a really good scrub and a coat of paint, it would be fine.'

He stared at her in astonishment, and realised she was serious. Absolutely serious, and so he looked again at the house, and realised with an equal degree of astonishment that she was right. It was dirty, it was dated and things like the curtains and wallpaper and lampshades made it all seem much more dreadful than it was.

But a coat of paint, some new carpets and curtains and a few pictures on the walls and it could be transformed.

'I had a survey done before the auction, and the wiring and plumbing are both sound,' he said slowly. 'The Aga's awful—'

'No!' she protested. 'Ben, I *love* the Aga!'

'What—that one? Solid fuel and probably temperamental as hell?'

She weakened. 'Well, maybe not that one.'

'So, a new Aga and a new bathroom suite, and we could probably manage for a while. And that way we could be in by Christmas. Even in time for the wedding.'

Her eyes widened, and her mouth made a round O before the tears welled up and she shut her mouth, clamping down on her lips to hold back the tears. It didn't work, and he laughed softly and wiped them away.

'Silly old you.'

'I just— If we could be in here before the baby—it would be so fantastic.'

'I'll give it my best shot. They owe me some leave. I'll take a bit now, and you can have some as well, to put your feet up—'

'What, while you're here painting the house? I don't think so! I'll be painting, too.'

'No, you won't,' he said firmly, meaning it. 'I don't need to be worrying about you inhaling fumes and wobbling about on ladders. You can sleep in in the mornings, and if you're very good you can bring me over a picnic at lunchtime and we can eat it together and I'll let you tell me I'm wonderful, and then you can go off and choose carpets and things for an hour before you go back to lie on my sofa and watch daytime TV.'

She wrinkled her nose, and he wanted to kiss it. 'I hate daytime TV,' she said, and he laughed.

'So spend the time planning the wedding,' he suggested, and she sighed.

'Oh, Ben. Do you think he'll come?'

He took her hand in his and rubbed the back of it absently. 'I don't know. Whatever happens, I'll be there, come hell or high water. But you have to talk to him, Lucy, or I will, because he needs to know, and he needs to come to terms with my role in your mother's death, because if I have anything to do with it, your father's going to be there at our wedding, and he's going to give you to me with his blessing. Now, come on, let's get out of here and find some lunch, and we probably need to start planning this wedding.'

He pulled her into his arms, gave her a quick hug and steered her towards the door.

CHAPTER NINE

THEY went to the Smugglers' Inn for a late lunch, up on the cliff near the church, and talked to the landlord, Tony, about booking a room for the day of the wedding.

'Just a small lunch party,' Lucy said, being deliberately vague.

'How many?' Tony asked, and she looked at Ben helplessly and shrugged.

'I don't know. Twenty, at the most?'

'Probably,' Ben agreed. 'I don't know. We need to make a definitive list yet, but would it be possible in principle?'

'Oh, yes. Mondays aren't busy. Want to see our buffet menu? It's very popular for weddings.'

She felt herself colouring. 'Is that your usual party fare?' she asked, refusing to answer the question in his eyes, but he just smiled and handed her the menu.

'Just have a look through,' he said, and pushed himself away from the bar. 'Now, let me get you a drink and you can sit down and browse through that and draw up your list over lunch. Are you ready to order?'

'Mmm—scampi and chips,' she said without hesitation. 'I love it here.'

'And for you, sir?'

'I'll have the same. And something non-alcoholic, times two. Lucy?'

'Oh—apple juice, please, Tony. Thanks.'

'Make that two.'

Tony set them on the bar. 'Here you go—look, there's a table by the fire. Go and warm yourselves and I'll bring the food over to you.'

'So—who's coming?' Ben asked softly once they were settled, pulling a notepad out of his pocket and flipping to a clean page.

She looked up at him, doubts flooding her. 'I don't know. My father, if I can persuade him. Jack, my twin, but I haven't spoken to him for ages and I know he's really busy, so he may not be able to get here on a weekday. Ed's in Africa, so he can't come. Marco and Dragan, although someone will have to be at work, I suppose. Kate, of course, and Chloe, my midwife, and Lauren, the physio, and Alison—she's a practice nurse and we've worked together a lot on the minor surgery. Melinda—the vet, you remember her, you stitched her arm. Vicky, the hairdresser—she'll do my hair, too, if I ask her. Gosh, I don't know. Mike and Fran Trevellyan? Mike's family bought the land from my grandmother's family donkey's years ago, and they live just up the road from Tregorran House. They'll be our closest neighbours, and I've known Mike since my childhood. I used to think he was gorgeous—he was my hero, and he put up with us trailing around after him with amazing patience. They've got a farm shop, and he runs the farmer's market here every Saturday. Fran's a teacher—so she may not be able to make it because she'll be at school, I expect. And, of course, Hazel and Sue and Doris from the surgery. How many's that?'

'Fifteen, if everyone comes. If your father and Jack and either Marco or Dragan and Fran can't make it, eleven.'

'What about you?'

'My parents—they're only in Tavistock, so that's not a problem. They're both working, but I'm sure they'll take the time off. My brother, Rob, and his wife, Polly? They're in London, so I expect they'll come down and stay with my parents for the weekend. Rob can be my best man. Jo, my registrar? A couple of other work colleagues. We can always have a big party later on, after the baby's born and we're settled in. Maybe a big christening in the summer.'

By which time, she thought, her father might have mellowed a little, Ed might be back from Africa and if she gave him enough notice, even Jack might manage to be there.

'Good idea,' she said with a smile. She picked up the notepad. 'That's somewhere between twenty and twenty-five, including us. Good guess. What about this menu?'

'What, the party food?' he teased, handing her the wedding buffet menu Tony had given them to look at, and she laughed awkwardly.

'I don't want to put it around the village until I've spoken to my father,' she said.

Tony came over at that moment and put their meals down and said in a low voice, 'I think you should know you were seen coming out of the Vicarage earlier, and the people of this village have always been good at adding two and two. If you're hoping to keep it a secret, you're in the wrong place, my friends. You've been well and truly rumbled.'

They exchanged rueful looks, and then the significance of it hit Lucy.

'Oh, Ben, I'm going to have to talk to my father now, before anybody else does.'

He put out a hand and stopped her. 'No. Eat your lunch, and we'll go together in a minute. Tony, lunch for twenty-five max from this menu will be lovely. Thank you.'

He handed it back to the landlord, who nodded, patted Lucy on the shoulder and said, 'Don't worry. We'll look after you. Everyone's delighted.'

Everyone except her father. And she still had to find out quite how undelighted he was.

He wouldn't even talk to her.

'I haven't got time to see you,' he said curtly when she went into his consulting room anyway, leaving Ben outside. 'Besides, I thought you said everything that was necessary last night. You've made it clear where your affections lie, so I suggest you get on with it.'

'Oh, Dad, please,' she said, her eyes filling. She blinked the tears away furiously, knowing they would only irritate him, and tried again. 'I love him. I know you think he was responsible—'

'No. I *know* he was responsible, and I'm having nothing more to do with either of you. You've made your bed, Lucy. Go and lie in it.'

She recoiled in shock, hardly able to believe how much he'd changed from the busy but caring parent he had been in her childhood. When had he turned into this man she didn't even know? She tried again. 'Dad, please. I want you to come to the wedding. I need you there. I can't get married without either of you—'

'That's your choice. And you've made it. You're marrying

a man who hasn't even got the guts to come with you and talk to me. Well, he's welcome to you. You deserve each other. Now I have a surgery, patients waiting, and I don't need this. Please go.'

She stood there for a moment longer, unbearably torn, but he ignored her pointedly, and in the end she stumbled through the door into Ben's arms. She hadn't let him come in with her, hoping it would help to soften her father, but it hadn't. It had made it worse.

'I'm going to talk to him,' Ben said, his voice shaking with anger, but she stopped him.

'No. Just get me out of here. I've had enough.'

He took her out to the car, opened the door for her, helped her in and closed the door, then disappeared. She looked round over her shoulder and saw him going back inside.

Oh, no! He was going to cause a scene...

He came back out again, opened his door and slid behind the wheel, then started the engine. 'I just told Kate you're taking next week off. She's arranging cover.' He shot her a quick glance, his eyes troubled. 'Are you all right?'

She couldn't hold it in any longer. Pressing her hand to her mouth, she shook her head, then burst into tears.

He swore, softly but comprehensively, and drove her home, then held her until she'd finally cried herself out. Then he made her a hot drink, tucked her up in bed and left her to sleep.

She didn't think she'd be able to, but she was exhausted by emotion, devastated by her father's rejection, and sleep promised oblivion. She closed her eyes, snuggled down on Ben's pillow, inhaling the scent of him, and finally dropped off to sleep.

* * *

'I can't believe it! She actually had the gall to ask me to go to her wedding!'

Kate sighed and closed the door of her office. Nick was pacing like a caged lion, the emotions chasing one after the other across his tortured face, and she didn't know what to say to him. She never did these days, and certainly not about this. Not about Annabel's death, but Ben didn't deserve this, and Lucy certainly didn't, and she couldn't just let it go.

'Why are you punishing your daughter because you feel guilty for letting Annabel down?' she asked softly, hitting right at the heart of it, and he stopped pacing and glared at her.

'I what?'

'You heard me. Annabel's death was nothing to do with Ben, and you know it. And you really can't go around accusing him of rigging the inquiry in public—unless you want to end up in court,' she added, getting into her stride. 'You've got to get a grip, Nick. She's been in love with Ben for years, since before Annabel died, and he's in love with her. This has been a long time coming, and with the baby on the way, it's not a moment too soon. I can't let you ruin her day for her, or her marriage, or her joy at becoming a mother. Just think about this, Nick. What would Annabel have had to say about your behaviour?'

And with that she walked out, shaking with anger and a whole range of other emotions she really didn't want to confront, and left him to think about it. Maybe when he'd cooled off and the dust had settled he'd change his mind, but she really didn't think he would.

The chances of him going to Lucy's wedding were slim to none, and Kate's heart ached for her.

* * *

Ben had to go to work on Sunday. He was on call, and he couldn't get out of it, but he hated leaving Lucy.

It was as if all the light had gone out of her, and he was furious with her father and worried sick about her. She'd even talked about calling off the wedding, but he'd managed to convince her it was silly. The wedding wasn't about her father, it was about their love and commitment for each other, and he was damned if Nick was going to screw up something so important because of his foolish and stiff-necked refusal to recognise the truth.

And then he ended up having to call him, because they had three people, a couple and a man on his own, presenting with similar symptoms of violent stomach cramps, acute nausea and vomiting and profuse diarrhoea, all within three hours of each other, and although the couple were from Exeter and the man from Birmingham, they had one thing in common—they'd all been staying at Trevallyn House in Penhally.

Damn. Ben didn't want to speak to him, and he was sure it was mutual, but he cut straight to the point. 'Dr Tremayne, I'm phoning from St Piran. It's Ben Carter—there's an outbreak of vomiting and diarrhoea that may be connected to Trevallyn House in Harbour Road in Penhally. It's run by—'

'Beatrice Trevallyn. I know. What are the symptoms?'

'Acute abdominal cramps, profuse diarrhoea—in one of the patients it's bloody and mucoid—vomiting, headache, pyrexia of 38.5°C. The first patient in is a man from Birmingham who stayed there last night, the other couple have been there since Friday and were on their way home. They became ill just after they started their journey. There are no other links that we can establish between them apart from Trevallyn House.'

'Right. I'll check it out. Have you notified Public Health?'

'No, I'm just about to. I suspect it's salmonella, and Public Health will want to inspect the premises. I'm just alerting you as it's likely you'll be called by anyone local who may be suffering from it. If it's not restricted to that one source, we need to know so we can set up an isolation unit.'

'Fine. I'll get on it now.'

And Nick hung up without another word. Ben shrugged. It suited him. The last thing he could envisage with the man was small talk!

He went back to the patients, isolated together in one bay, and concentrated on getting fluids into them and monitoring their symptoms. They were all too ill to travel home, and until they got the results of the stool samples from the Public Health lab, they needed to be barrier nursed in isolation. The last thing they needed in the hospital was an outbreak of winter vomiting virus, and the symptoms were similar.

He set up IV fluid replacement, checked them all again to make sure there was no further deterioration, and then he was vomited on.

Great.

He went and showered very, very thoroughly. He didn't need to take home anything nasty to a pregnant woman who already had quite enough on her plate.

'Call for you, Ben,' the charge nurse said through the door. 'It's Nick Tremayne.'

'Take a message,' he yelled, and towelled himself roughly dry, pulled on a clean set of scrubs and went back out. 'What did he want?'

'Mrs Trevallyn is sick, and her son, Davey, is in a state of collapse—he's got learning difficulties as well, by the way.

He's sending them in. He says there are no other residents, nobody else has been there in the last seventy-two hours and he hasn't been called out by anyone from outside the guest house.'

'Right. Thanks. Looks localised, then. Anything from Public Health?'

'No. I'll chase them up.'

'Do that—and can we get these three up to a medical ward? All five can be nursed together, and if I'm right, that'll be the end of it, unless it's meat from a local supplier, in which case we could get many more.'

'Look on the bright side, why don't you,' the charge nurse said with a grin, and went to organise the removal of their patients from the unit.

'I'll get a fleet of cleaners in to deal with this lot,' he threw over his shoulder. 'We'll need a serious hosing-down of all this contaminated equipment before we can put it back into use.'

'Good idea.'

And he needed to phone Lucy. He couldn't leave the department until he had the results back and was sure it was only a restricted salmonella outbreak and not something much worse and more widespread.

It was the best and yet the most appalling fortnight of Lucy's life. If it hadn't been for Ben, it would have been intolerable—but if it hadn't been for Ben, it wouldn't have been intolerable, so that was stupid.

After Sunday when he was at work, they spent a lot of time together, both at Tregorran House and in his old house in Orchard Way. She was having only three days off, and refused to take any more despite Ben's persuasion, so she had to make the best of it. And they were lovely days.

She wasn't allowed to do anything, but he couldn't stop her planning, and she ordered a skip and watched him fill it with the horrible carpets and curtains, and made notes for the wedding.

Not that there were many to make.

She needed a dress. She needed flowers—a simple posy would do, nothing much, and as it was Advent the church wouldn't have flowers. Foliage, then—ivy and eucalyptus and variegated laurel from the garden. She could see plenty of things from where she was sitting, and if she had a few white flowers interspersed—roses, perhaps?—that would be enough.

The food was taken care of, and the drinks they'd get from Tony, and she'd spoken to everyone except Jack and Ed. Ed she'd emailed, because it was the easiest way to deal with it, and she'd sent Jack a text.

Needless to say, he hadn't called her back, but he was obviously up to his eyes. He was working hard, throwing himself into his career—although to hear her father on the subject you'd be forgiven for thinking he was never out of nightclubs—and she knew he'd get back to her when he could.

As for the rest—well, there was no 'rest'. That was it, the sum total of the arrangements. The hymns were chosen, the order of service typed up on Ben's computer and printed off on fine card, and there was nothing left to do but wait for Jack to ring and her father to come round.

She wasn't holding her breath.

'You OK?'

She smiled up at Ben. 'I'm fine. How about you?'

'Good. All done. The skip's full, the house is empty, all

ready for the decorators to come in and blitz it, and guess what I found?'

He dangled a big old iron key in front of her, and she exclaimed in delight and reached for it. 'The front door key!'

'Is it? I thought it might be. It was under the mat. Want to try it?'

'Oh, yes. I expect it'll be a bit rusty, but we used to go out into the garden in the summer through the front door. It's got bolts as well—I'll let you do those.'

So he struggled with the bolts and finally freed them, and she put the key in the lock and turned it, and although it was a bit stiff, they heard the lock go, and together they turned the doorknob. A gust of wind caught the door and blew it open, and in front of them, beyond the garden and the field, was the sea, sparkling in the low winter sunlight.

She filled her lungs with the cold, fresh air and laughed. 'Oh, that's gorgeous! Oh, Ben, thank you.'

'What, for finding the key? We could have had another one made.'

'No,' she said, turning to him and cradling his face in her hands. 'For getting me my house.'

He stared down at her in silence for a moment, then he sighed softly and drew her into his arms.

'It's a pleasure,' he murmured. 'Just to see you happy is more than enough reward.'

He let her go, lifting his head, then he said, 'Is that your phone?'

'Oh—yes. I'll get it.' She hurried to her bag and pulled it out, pressing the button just in time. 'Hello?'

'Hi, kiddo.'

'Jack! Oh, Jack, I'm so glad you've got back to me. You got my text?'

'Yes, I got it. That's why I'm ringing you.'

'Tell me you can come,' she pleaded. 'Dad's being really difficult—it's because it's Ben. He's still being really stupid about it and I can't get through to him. I don't think there's a prayer he'll come to the wedding, and Ed's in Africa—Jack, I want you to give me away.'

There was a lengthy silence, and her heart sank. 'Jack?'

'Ah, hell, Lucy. Oh, God, I'm so sorry, kiddo, I can't. Did you hear India died?'

'Yes, of course I did. It was in all the gossip rags. Not that you told me, of course, because you never tell me anything—'

'She's got a child,' he cut in.

'Yes, I saw. But—'

'Lucy, he's mine. His name's Freddie, and—he's my son. I've been granted custody of him, and—oh, sis, I need you. I'm just so out of my depth. I don't know what I'm doing with him.'

She walked back into the kitchen and sat down again at the table they'd set up in there. 'Oh, Jack. I don't believe it. How old is he?'

'Um—little. Nearly three. I'm just— I'm having problems with him adjusting to me. He misses his mother, and he doesn't know who the hell I am, and I really don't think I can leave him right now, and I certainly can't bring him, not all that way. And all the fuss would just confuse him more.'

He wasn't coming. And he was a father! Much more important, she told herself, and set aside her disappointment.

'Oh, Jack, I quite understand. Don't beat yourself up over it. And remember, you're not alone. We're all here for you. You could move back down here, so we can all help you.'

'I can't see Dad helping. He'd say I brought it on myself.'

'No,' she said, but with more conviction than she felt. 'He'll come round.'

'I wish I had your confidence. Oh, Lucy, I just don't know how to deal with Freddie—what to say to him to make it better.'

'Just put yourself in his position, and be there for him, and be kind. And think about what I said, about moving back here. You don't have to do this by yourself.'

He gave a ragged laugh that broke in the middle. 'Just at the moment I don't know if I can do it at all, sis. You know, give me a job I can do—a really messy RTA with lots of reconstruction work—and I'm happy as a pig in muck. Give me a little boy with huge blue eyes that watch me warily all day long, and I just fall apart. He needs a mother, and his own was bloody useless but at least she loved him...'

His voice cracked, and Lucy's heart ached for him. For both of them. 'Oh, Jack, you'll cope,' she said gently. 'If I wasn't so pregnant I'd come and see you, but—'

'No, don't be silly. You marry your Ben, and I'll be thinking of you at the time, but I can't get down. I'm so, so sorry.'

'Don't be. You're doing the right thing. Give him a hug from his Aunty Lucy, and you take care. I'll send you both a bit of cake.'

'You do that—and have a really great day. Love you, kiddo.'

'Love you too, big bro.'

She lowered the phone to her lap and looked up at Ben, her heart heavy. 'He can't come. He's got a son—Freddie. He's only just found out, and he's having problems with him and can't leave him. There won't be anybody in my family there, Ben. Not one.'

'Oh, darling…'

He gathered her into his arms and cradled her close, his heart breaking for her. And then the baby kicked him, and he lifted his head and smiled down at her. 'That's not true. I'll be there, and so will the baby. I don't know if it's enough, but we're your family, too, and we'll be there. So you won't be alone.'

Her hands slid down and cradled the baby, and a tear slipped down her cheek, catching on her lip as she smiled. 'No. I won't. You're right. And you're all I need—all I'll ever need.'

Kate knocked briefly on Nick's consulting-room door and walked in.

He was standing at the window, his jaw set, arms folded, and a muscle twitched in his cheek.

'Nick?'

'I'm not going.'

'Why?'

He turned, letting out his breath in an explosive sigh. 'You know why.'

She couldn't let him do this. She couldn't let him miss his own daughter's wedding because when he came to his senses it would be another layer of guilt to add to the countless others.

'You have to go. This isn't about you, it's about Lucy, and it's about her mother.'

'Her *dead* mother.'

'Exactly. Her mother who can't be there for her. Her mother who can't sit just over her left shoulder, sniffing into a handkerchief and being ridiculously proud of her. Lucy's not asking you to give her away, and neither am I. Mike Trevellyan's doing it. She just wants you there, in the congregation, so she's not the only one there from the Tremayne family.'

'He let her die.'

'No. No, he didn't, Nick. He did everything he could, and he was gutted that she died. And he loves Lucy to bits. He'll be a good husband and father. He'll make her happy—which is more than you're doing at the moment. So—are you coming, or not?'

For a moment she thought he'd say no, but then he snatched his coat off the back of the door, shrugged into it and yanked the door open. 'Well, come on, then, we don't want to be late.'

Nick couldn't believe he was doing it.

Going to Lucy's wedding, in the church where his father and brother and Annabel had all been laid to rest.

He nearly turned round and drove back, but Kate wouldn't have let him and, anyway, she was right. He had to be there, for Lucy's mother.

The church car park was full, to his surprise, and he had to go to the Smugglers' Inn. It was only a few yards further, but as they hurried back, he saw Lucy arriving in Mike Trevellyan's wonderful old car. It was done up with ribbons, and it was gleaming, and as Mike helped her out, Nick's footsteps faltered.

He should be doing that. Giving her away. Not some man who was almost a stranger.

He broke into a run, Kate after him, and they reached the church just as the music started and she was walking down the aisle.

'Here,' Kate said, tucking a flower into his buttonhole, and she gave him a little shove.

The vicar was there in his ceremonial robes, Ben standing ramrod straight in front of him, and when he turned to look at Lucy, his eyes met Nick's and held. Then he looked down into Lucy's face and smiled.

* * *

'He's here,' Ben said.

'Who?'

'Your father.'

She turned, searching the crowd, but then she saw him, hesitating at the back of the church, as if he was unsure of his welcome. He smiled at her, a sad, twisted smile, and she held out her hand, but he didn't move.

For an endless moment everyone held their breath, and then she gave up, and turned back to the vicar. Ben's hand caught hers and tightened on it, giving her support, and she clung to him.

Her father was here. He'd said he wouldn't come, but he was here. Mike was hovering beside her, unsure what to do, but she smiled at the vicar and nodded, and he smiled back.

'Dearly beloved,' he began, and Lucy listened and tried to concentrate, but then, when Mr Kenner said, 'Who gives this woman to be married to this man?' there was a ripple through the congregation, and her father's voice rang out.

'I do,' he said, and reaching her side he took her right hand, kissed her cheek and said softly, 'I'm sorry,' and placed her hand in Ben's.

CHAPTER TEN

BEN wasn't sure he could believe it.

After all the agonising and trauma of the past two weeks, he'd come, in the end, and given his daughter away.

And his eyes, as he'd placed her hand in Ben's, had held a challenge that should probably have struck fear into Ben's heart.

It didn't, because it was a challenge he had every intention of meeting. He was going to make Lucy happy if it took his last breath, and he didn't need Nick Tremayne to challenge him to do it.

And Lucy *was* happy.

Her face shone, her eyes were bright, and she'd never looked more beautiful. And when she paused outside the church and walked over to her mother's grave and laid a single white rose from her bouquet in front of the simple headstone, her eyes sparkled with tears, and he was sure his did, too.

He didn't know about Nick. He wasn't looking at him, he had eyes only for Lucy, and as they made their way to the Smugglers' Inn, it seemed as if the whole of Penhally had turned out to shower them with good wishes.

Ben chuckled to himself. They might be the most phenomenal load of old busybodies, but they were there because they loved Lucy, and he couldn't blame them for that.

He recognised several of the faces in the crowd gathered on the clifftop—Toby Penhaligan, the fisherman with the broken arm, Bea Trevallyn from the guesthouse with the salmonella outbreak, fortunately contained to just the five identified, and others such as Mrs Lunney, with her new husband Henry, who'd come all the way from Wadebridge just to cheer them as they came out of the church.

It was touching, and as they walked away, Lucy tucked her hand tighter into the crook of his arm and smiled up at him.

'He came.'

'I know.' But he was worried, and he said softly, 'Lucy, don't expect too much. One step at a time.'

She nodded. 'I know. Early days. But one step, today, is enough for me.'

The pub was packed.

They'd booked a room for up to twenty-five, and it should have been enough, but so many people had come to wish them well, and her father asked the landlord to give them all a drink in celebration.

'Ouch. That'll cost him,' she said with a smile, and Ben chuckled.

'I don't think he'll mind. Come on, we need to stand here and greet everyone.'

As a reception line, it was a strange affair, oddly formal in the rather informal and yet curiously fitting surroundings of the pub.

Her father, Ben's parents—lovely, lovely people who'd

been so sweet to her in the last two weeks—his brother, Rob, just like him in many ways, his sister-in-law, Polly, who she was looking forward to getting to know much, much better, and hovering in the background organising, as ever, was Kate.

Dear Kate, who must have talked her father into coming, because without her Lucy was sure he wouldn't have come.

She greeted her with a heartfelt hug and a whispered, 'Thanks.'

Kate smiled back and mouthed, 'Any time,' and then moved on down the line, followed by all the others.

Neither Marco nor Dragan had come, both electing to hold the fort to make sure Nick had no plausible excuses, she was sure, but apart from Sue who was manning the reception desk and Alison Myers who had a baby clinic, the rest of the staff were there, and Ben's colleagues, and after them, it seemed, came the whole of Penhally, so many of them, come to wish her and Ben well.

And get plastered on the doctor's slate.

There wouldn't be a lot of work done in Penhally that afternoon, she thought, and wondered how many more people were going to hug and kiss her before she could go and sit down…

Nick hated speeches, and this was one he'd never intended to make, so it was short and to the point.

'I've never seen my daughter look so radiant,' he said. 'And her mother, who should have been here, would have been so, so proud of her. And on her behalf, I'd like to wish you every happiness. Ben, take care of her. Love her well. And may you be as happy as we were. Ladies and gentlemen, the bride and groom.'

And he drained his glass, sat down and took a deep, steadying breath. He didn't like Ben, and he didn't intend to spend time in his company, but Lucy apparently loved him, and after all he didn't have to live with the man. And today, on their wedding day, he wasn't going to fight with him.

Nick reached for the bottle of champagne and refilled his glass. He only lived at the bottom of the hill. He could walk home. It was his daughter's wedding day, and everybody was having too much to drink. He was damned if he wasn't going to join them...

'Ben, why are we here?'

'Just humour me,' he said. 'Stay there.'

Lucy paused, her dress caught up in her hand so it didn't trail in the dirt, and Ben disappeared round the side of the house, came back a moment later, scooped her up in his arms and carried her, laughing, round to the other side of the house and in through the front door.

'You're crazy. What are you doing?' she said breathlessly, then realised, and her heart lodged in her throat. He was carrying her over the threshold.

'There,' he said, sliding her carefully to her feet. 'You wouldn't let me do it before we were married, but there's no excuse now. Welcome home, Mrs Carter.'

'Thank you.' She went up on tiptoe and kissed him, still laughing, then looked around and gasped. She hadn't been allowed in the house for days, and she'd spent last night at her flat, getting ready this morning with Chloe and Lauren to help her.

But now...

'It's furnished!' she exclaimed. 'How? When?'

'Today. The removal men had strict instructions, and hope-fully they've done everything right. I'm sure they won't have done, and we'll have to move all sorts of stuff, but I wanted to bring my bride home—to our real home.'

'Oh, Ben,' she said, lost for words. Taking him by the hand, she went from room to room. 'Oh, it's lovely. Oh! The nursery! Oh, Ben, you've had it painted in just the right colours.'

'*I* painted it,' he said, following her into the room she'd used as a child. 'I wanted to do it myself. For the baby.'

'Oh, Ben,' she said again, and then she couldn't talk any more. She just threw herself into his arms and hugged him so hard she thought she could hear his ribs creak.

'Is it OK? Do you like it?'

But she could only nod, because the tears were clogging her throat and she just couldn't believe how much he'd achieved in so short a time.

'I take it that's a yes,' he said with a laugh, and hugged her back, rather more gently. 'Come on, you haven't see our bed-room yet.'

And he led her up the corridor and opened the door. A beautiful old French sleigh bed took pride of place opposite the window, positioned just where she'd be able to sit up in bed and look at the sea. It was made up with fresh, crisp white linen, the duvet a cloud of goosedown, and piled with pillows just right for propping herself up to take advantage of the view.

It also looked hugely inviting.

She was tired. It had been a long day and was hard on the heels of a night when she hadn't slept a wink.

'How do you fancy trying it out?' he asked, drawing her back against him. 'I missed you last night, and I didn't sleep at all.'

'Neither did I.' She turned in his arms and smiled. 'I think trying it out sounds wonderful. Take me to bed, Mr Carter— please?'

He chuckled. 'Since you ask so nicely,' he said.

They couldn't take any time off.

Because it was so close to Christmas, they both had to go back to work on Tuesday morning, and it was a real effort to drag themselves out of the blissfully comfortable embrace of their new bed.

Ben had to leave earlier than Lucy, and after he'd gone she wandered around the house, touching it, remembering. 'I wonder what you'd make of it, Grannie?' she murmured. 'I hope you're happy that we're here. We'll look after it, and love it, and love each other and our children just as you did. You can rest now.'

Gosh, such sentimental nonsense. She blinked hard and went into the kitchen to make herself another cup of tea before she had to leave. The old Aga was still there, and there was a six-week wait for a new one, but she didn't mind. There was something curiously comforting about the sight of it, and Ben had promised her he'd try and get it going for Christmas. In the meantime there was a rather elderly electric stove standing next to the fridge, but it would do.

She drank her tea, washed up the mug—a novelty, that, not having a dishwasher, she'd got rather used to Ben's—and went to work.

Wow. Christmas Eve.

She'd done her Christmas shopping on Saturday, with Ben, and the presents were wrapped and under the tree in the sitting room—all except for the fire dogs she'd bought him from the salvage yard to put in the big granite fireplace in the sitting room. They'd been hiding in the boot of her car under a blanket until she'd struggled to heave them out that morning after Ben had gone, but they were a bit heavy for her to lift and she'd had to tuck them round the corner of the little stone barn beside the house. Her father had been hard to buy for. What could you give a man who didn't seem to connect with life any more?

Not at any real level. Even after the wedding, he'd still been distant, and any hopes she might have cherished that they were back to normal had been dashed when she'd asked him to join them at the house for Christmas Day, the following Tuesday.

'I'm going to Kate's,' he'd said. 'Sorry. Can't let her down. But I'm sure you'll have a lovely day.'

'Can't you come for some of it? Bring Kate and Jem—come for a drink, or tea, or something.'

'Sorry, Lucy.'

And that had been that. So she'd bought him a bottle of a fine single malt whiskey and a Christmas cake and a pot of Stilton, and put them in a wicker basket, and it was under her desk at the moment waiting for a chance to give it to him. Dull, boring but safe, she thought, and wondered if he'd be disappointed. No more than he was disappointed in her, she was sure.

Oh, well. She didn't have time to worry about it. She had a surgery until ten, and then two minor ops booked in, one the removal of a sebaceous cyst on the back of a man's neck, the other a seborrhoeic keratosis, harmless but irritating and looking troubling like a melanoma to the uninitiated.

She was examining it, reassuring herself about her initial diagnosis, when she noticed Ben's car pull up in the car park.

What was he doing here?

She forced herself to concentrate, and infiltrated the area in the man's armpit with local anaesthetic, listening to his stream of inconsequential chatter and putting in the odd remark from time.

'Oh, I've got a message for you from Mrs Pearce, Mrs Jones's neighbour. She says to tell you Edith's doing really well and hopes to be home in a week or two.'

'Oh, good. I'll go and see her when I'm next at St Piran. Right, is that numb now?'

'Yes—can't feel a thing.'

'OK.' She curetted it off, cauterised the wound and dressed it with antibiotic cream and a non-adherent dressing. 'Right, keep it dry if you can, put the cream on twice a day, leave it uncovered once it stops being sore and in two to three weeks it should be gone. It'll just look and feel like a burn, and that's what it is, really, because I've singed the blood vessels to seal them. OK?'

'What about that thing?' He pointed at the flat brown blob of tissue she'd removed and put in a specimen tube.

'I'll send it for analysis, just to be on the safe side, but I'm absolutely confident that it's harmless.'

'So you're sending it off so I can't sue you?'

She chuckled. 'No, I'm sending it off because I want to know that I've done everything I should have for you. I'm only a doctor, I don't have all the answers. And I don't want to let you down.'

He nodded. 'Fair enough. Thank you very much.'

He left, and she thought about it. Would she send the

sample off just so she didn't get sued if it later turned out to be a melanoma? Or was it belt and braces?

The latter. Being sued would be horrible, but the chances were it would happen in her working lifetime. Being responsible for someone's death because she hadn't taken enough care—that was quite different. It would destroy you, unless you simply didn't have a conscience.

She felt a twinge—nothing much, just another of those wretched Braxton Hicks contractions that she'd been plagued with for ages. Still, she was finished now, and she wasn't due back to work until Thursday. And Ben was here. He must have popped in to see her, but she had to get the sample off.

She was just coming out of her consulting room with the histology sample in her hand when she overheard his voice coming through her father's open consulting-room door.

'Please, come—not for me, but for Lucy. Even if it's just for a drink. She's so disappointed that we won't see you.'

'Well, that's her fault, not mine. She knows where I'll be, and it won't be with you. Just because I was at the wedding doesn't mean I've forgiven you or changed my mind about you. I only went to the wedding for Lucy, and for Annabel. I gave her away because I couldn't break her heart, but I don't have to like it, or you, and if you've got any ideas about cosy little suppers and so forth you can just forget it, because frankly even one minute in your company is one minute too long. You've taken my family home, taken my daughter, taken my wife—'

'No!' Ben cut in, his voice firm, and Lucy sagged against her open door, wondering if this was ever going to stop. 'I didn't take the house, I bought the house at a fair market price at an open auction because I thought it would make your daughter happy, and I didn't take Lucy, she came to me because she loves me and knows I love her and I didn't take your wife, Tremayne. On the contrary, I did everything I could to save her once she came to my attention.'

'That's a lie!' Nick said furiously. 'You gave up on her! I saw you!'

'I know. And you shouldn't have done. But we didn't give up. We stopped, simply because she was already dead. Her pupils were blown, her heart had stopped beating thirty minutes before. She was dead, Nick. She was dead, and if I could have changed that, for you, for her, for Lucy, don't you think I would have done so? But I never, ever gave up on her while there was the slightest chance of saving her.'

'She should have gone to Theatre.'

'There wasn't one free—and there wasn't time. So we did what we could, and we failed. And I'm sorry. But it's not my fault. If you want someone to blame, I suggest you look a little closer to home!'

'Just what the hell are you implying?'

'I'm not implying anything. I'm telling you that if it was anyone's fault she died, it was yours, because you were too busy building your empire to notice that the woman you supposedly loved was so sick she was overdosing on painkillers because she didn't want to trouble you! And that is why she died.'

Lucy gasped, and behind Reception Hazel and Kate stood transfixed.

The door slammed back against the wall and Ben stormed out, his face taut with anger. The noise of the door seemed to free them, and Lucy sagged against the doorframe, utterly shocked at the terrible things that had been said. Kate hurried towards her. 'Lucy—oh, my dear, I'm so sorry. Come and sit down.'

'No. I have to talk to him. He can't…'

She walked through her father's door on legs of jelly, and found him throwing books out of his bookcase, searching through them and discarding them furiously.

'Dad?'

'I'm going to sue him. I'm sorry, I know he's your husband now, but I can't let him get away with that.'

'What if he's right?'

He froze, then glared at her, his eyes suddenly ice cold. 'Get out,' he said flatly. 'If that's what you think, get out, and go home to him. I don't want to see you again!'

'Nick, really, this is ridiculous—' Kate interjected.

'Fine, I'll go,' Lucy sobbed. Turning, she ran back past Kate to her consulting room and grabbed her handbag. The histology bottle was still in her hand, and she gave it to Hazel on the way out. 'Um, could you send that for histology, please? Thank you. And—happy Christmas,' she added, before, blinded by tears, she ran out to the car, climbed awkwardly behind the wheel and drove out.

The roads were slick with rain, and as she drove towards Tregorran House and Ben, the rain turned to sleet and then snow, swirling, blinding snow of the sort they rarely saw in Cornwall. It would be gone in a moment, but for now it was blinding her, mingling with the tears until she couldn't see.

She felt the jolt, felt the car slide, and then judder and tilt alarmingly before coming to rest, the engine still running.

Oh, God, no, she thought. Phone. Where's the phone? Got to call Ben. Bag. Where is it?

In the footwell. Her bag was in the passenger footwell, right over on the far side and she suddenly understood the meaning of the expression heavily pregnant. She was hanging in her seat belt, leaning towards the passenger side, and she just couldn't quite— Got it!

And it was wet. Very wet, and as she watched the water rose further, and the car shifted and settled lower into the ditch. She had to get out, but how?

Turn off the engine, she remembered. Turn off the engine. Creaks, hissing, bubbling—it was like something out of a horror movie. She wasn't even sure where she was, but she couldn't be far from home. A hundred yards? Two hundred?

She pushed the door with all her strength, and it lifted, then dropped back. Ben, she thought, and phoned him, but he was out of range.

Nine nine nine?

Or her father?

No. She wasn't hurt, she was just stuck. She sent Ben a text, and told him where she was, then took her seat belt off, manoeuvred herself round so she was kneeling on the seat with her feet braced on the handbrake and her head by the window, and she heaved the door up and out of the way, pushing it until it held on the stay.

Would it remain there? The car was only tilted, not on its side, so it might stay there long enough for her to scramble out. Especially if she wedged it with something. Something like her handbag, always too full of things but on this occasion usefully so. She jammed it under the bottom of the door, so at least it wouldn't slam on her, and then clambered awkwardly out into the swirling snow.

Why was it snowing? She slipped on the road surface and grabbed the door to save herself, then remembered her bag. It was squashed now, but nothing in there was important.

Except her phone.

Fingers trembling, she pulled it out and saw with horror that it was cracked. She tried to use it, but it didn't work.

As if it could get any worse, she thought a little hysterically, and then she felt another of those annoying contractions, but it wasn't just annoying, it was huge, painful, and very significant.

And then there was a warm, wet, rushing sensation down her legs.

'Oh, no. Ben, please come,' she mouthed silently. 'I can't do this on my own.'

She looked around her frantically, desperately searching for anything she could recognise, and then she spotted the barn, and her heart sank. She was at least half a mile from home, and she couldn't possibly walk that distance. She'd have to get back in the car, she thought, and wait for Ben, but then there was a creak, and a groan of tortured metal, and the car tilted further and slid down into the ditch.

So that took care of that.

It's a good job I took the fire dogs out, she thought, and then wondered how on earth she could worry about something so trivial when she was about to give birth on the roadside in a blizzard!

Another contraction hit her, and she sagged against the car, let it pass and then straightened up. She could get to the barn. It was only a few yards away—fifty at the most. It wouldn't be warm, but at least she'd be out of the snow and sleet, and she could sit down and wait for Ben.

Wherever he was. What if he didn't get the message? What if he didn't come?

She wrote, 'IN THE BARN' on the side of the car in the dirty snow, and hoped someone would come. Anyone.

And soon…

* * *

'"Had crash near home. Please come. L xxxx". Oh, my God.' Ben felt cold all over, sick and scared and useless. He'd been shopping—shopping, of all things!—and she'd had a car accident and been unable to reach him!

He dialled her mobile number, but it went straight to voice-mail. She might be calling someone else, he reasoned, so he left a message. 'I'm coming, sweetheart. Stay there. Don't move, and call an ambulance if you need to.'

And then, after a second's hesitation, he phoned the practice. Kate answered, sounding distracted and upset, and he wondered if it was a good idea, but it was better than leaving Lucy without help.

'Kate, it's Ben. I've had a text from Lucy to say she's had a car accident on her way back to the house. Have you heard from her?'

'No, but she was really upset. Ben, she heard the row.'

He swore, then thought for a moment. 'Kate, I'm worried. I can't get her. Her phone might not be working. Can you try and find her? I'm on my way but I might need help. She might have gone into labour—you're a midwife, aren't you?'

'Yes. Don't worry, we'll come. I'll bring a delivery pack just in case. And I'll call the ambulance. You just get to her.'

He drove fast—probably faster than was truly sensible, but not so fast that he was likely to end up in a ditch.

'Lucy!' He pulled up behind her car, ran to the door and yanked it open, but the car was empty, canted over at a crazy angle and filling with water. Hell. He dropped the door and looked round, then spotted the barn. Would she have gone there?

He looked around again, then noticed something on the side of the car. Writing. IN THE BA. Barn? The barn!

He wrote it again, clearing the fresh snow from the letters, and then got back in his car and shot down the road, pulling up outside in a slither of slush and gravel. 'Lucy!' he yelled, and he heard an answering sob.

'Ben! In here—I'm having the baby.'

Dear God. And he had nothing with him—no gloves, no sterile drapes, nothing to protect her from contamination. He ran into the barn and found her huddled against some straw bales, and gathered her, sobbing, into his arms. 'Are you hurt?'

'No—but the baby's coming, Ben. I can feel it—I can feel the head. It can't come now, I'm only thirty-four weeks! It's too early.'

'You'll be fine,' he said, giving her one last squeeze. 'There's an ambulance on the way, and I've called Kate, just in case. You stay there. I'm going to sort these bales out and then have a look at you.'

He stood up, shifted a few bales to make a flat, clean area of fresh straw, then stripped off his coat and laid it on them, scooped her up and set her down in the middle of it. 'We need to get these wet trousers off you,' he said, and peeled them down her legs, taking the tiny lacy knickers that he adored with them.

Hell. She was right. The baby's head was crowning, and there was no time to do anything except catch it.

'I want to push.'

'No. Just wait—if you can. Pant. Wait for Kate, she won't be long.'

'Lucy?'

'What's he doing here?'

'He's your father.'

'He didn't want to see me again.'

'Lucy?' Another bellow from Nick.

'In here,' Ben yelled, thinking that he'd never expected to be pleased to see Nick Tremayne, but, by God, he was. And Kate—dear, sensible Kate, who elbowed them both out of the way, thrust a delivery pack in Nick's hands and told him to unwrap it, sent Ben to hug Lucy up at the other end and took over.

'The cord's around its neck,' Kate said. 'Lucy, I'm just going to put my finger in and free it, then you can push again, darling, all right? Just hang on, just another minute, there's a good girl.'

She wriggled a loop of cord free, worked it over the baby's head, felt again, and then smiled. 'Right, my love. In your own time, when you feel the next contraction, just pant and push gently with your mouth open— That's it, lovely, nice and steady— Well done. Ben, can I have your jumper, please?'

He peeled it off over his head and handed it to her, and with the next contraction she delivered the baby onto the jumper, lifted it and laid it on Lucy's abdomen, tucking the warm fabric round it.

'I need to suck it out,' Kate said, taking the aspirator from Nick and clearing the baby's nose and mouth of mucus while Ben held his breath and prayed.

And then there was an indignant squall, and Lucy sobbed with relief, and he closed his eyes, hugged her close and wondered if he'd ever heard anything more beautiful in all his life.

'Well, I have to say, if you were going to have a baby in a stable at Christmas, you could have had a boy,' Kate murmured, and Lucy gave a fractured little laugh and peered in amazement at the baby.

'It's a girl?'

'Yes—yes, it's a girl,' Kate said gently. 'Congratulations.' She turned. 'Nick, could you go and flag down the ambulance? I can hear it coming.'

He turned and went without a word, but Ben caught a glimpse of his face, taut with emotion, and wished he could unsay the words he'd said that morning. However true.

'I love you,' Ben said, pressing a lingering kiss to his wife's brow, and she looked up at him, her eyes filled with wonder, and smiled.

'I love you, too. Oh, Ben, look at her, she's beautiful.'

She wasn't. She was streaked with blood and mucus, covered in the creamy vernix that protected her skin *in utero*, and her face was screwed up with indignation, and he'd never seen anything so amazing in all his life.

'Ben? Ben, can you get the door?'

Lucy was lying propped up in bed, the baby in her arms, and she didn't know where Ben was. He'd gone downstairs to start cooking their lunch some time ago, and there wasn't a sign of him.

'Ben?'

'I've got it,' he yelled, and she heard the front door creak open, and then silence.

Silence?

'Ben, who is it?' she called, but there was no reply, and she slipped out of bed and padded to the top of the stairs, the baby in her arms.

She could hear voices, but she couldn't hear what they were saying until she reached the end of the landing, and then she saw them. The big front door at the foot of the stairs was closed, and Ben and her father were standing there in front of it, talking in hushed tones.

'I'll quite understand if you want me to go.'

'No. No, I don't want you to go, Nick, but I'm not going to let you upset Lucy.'

'I won't. I promise. But I must see her—and you. I owe you both a massive apology. You were right—I neglected Annabel, and I didn't want to see it, so I made you the scapegoat. And I don't know how you can ever forgive me for that. It was unforgivable—'

'No, it wasn't. You were blinded by grief, and you were lashing out. I don't have that excuse. I was really hard on you—I said dreadful things, and I'm really sorry.'

'True things. I was busy with my empire.'

'No, you were busy setting up a vital community health centre, and you took your eye off the ball. We all do it. And really the fault, if any, was Annabel's for downplaying it too long. It was just one of those terrible things, Nick. I'm just so sorry that I couldn't do anything about it.'

'It wasn't your fault,' her father said, gruffly uttering the words Lucy had given up hoping he would say, and she must have made a noise because they both lifted their heads and looked up at her.

'Hello, Dad,' she said, and his face twisted.

'Hello, Lucy. Happy New Year. I've brought something for the baby.'

He seemed so uncertain, so uncharacteristically unsure and, tucking the baby more securely in her arm, she went carefully down the stairs and into his arms. 'Happy New Year,' she said softly, going up on tiptoe and kissing his cold cheek. 'Here—say hello to your granddaughter.'

He bent and touched her little face with a blunt fingertip, and his mouth compressed. 'She's lovely. May I hold her?'

'Of course. Ben, can you take Dad's coat? Come through to the sitting room, we've got the fire going.'

And she led him through into the room where he'd spent so much time in his own childhood, and there, in a chair by the fire, she settled him down and laid the baby in his arms.

'She's beautiful,' he said gruffly. 'Just like you were. Does she have a name yet?'

Ben came up beside her, one arm around her shoulders, holding her close. 'We thought—if you didn't mind—we'd like to call her Annabel.'

Nick's throat worked, and when he lifted his head, his eyes were filled with tears.

'I think Annabel would be a lovely name for her,' he said. 'A very fitting name. And I'm sure your mother would think so, too.' He cleared his throat. 'So—should we wet the baby's head?' he suggested. 'I brought you a bottle of champagne as a peace offering. Not much of one, but I thought you could always hit me over the head with it—it's nice and heavy.'

Ben laughed, dispersing the tension, and disappeared, coming back moments later with glasses. He opened the bottle with a soft pop and filled them, then lifted his glass.

'To Annabel,' he said, and her father's jaw tensed.

'To Annabel,' he echoed, and pressed a kiss lightly to the baby's forehead. 'Both of them.'

Lucy didn't speak. She just lifted the glass and touched the champagne to her lips. Just a tiny taste, because of her milk. And she thought of her mother, of the terrible bitterness of the last two years now finally laid to rest, and as Ben's arm came around her shoulders again, a tear slid down her cheek.

'To both of them,' she echoed softly.

BRIDES OF PENHALLY BAY

Medical™ is proud to welcome you to Penhally
Bay Surgery where you can meet the team led by
caring and commanding Dr Nick Tremayne.
For twelve months we will bring you an
emotional, tempting romance – devoted
doctors, single fathers, a sheikh surgeon,
royalty, blushing brides and miracle babies
that will warm your heart…

*Let us whisk you away to this Cornish coastal
town – to a place where hearts are made whole.*

Turn the page for a sneak preview from
The Italian's New Year Marriage Wish
by Sarah Morgan
– the second book in the
BRIDES OF PENHALLY BAY series.

THE ITALIAN'S NEW YEAR
MARRIAGE WISH
by
Sarah Morgan

'*Sì*, come in.'

The sound of his smooth, confident voice made her stomach lurch and she closed her eyes briefly. Despite his enviable fluency in English, no one could ever have mistaken Marco Avanti for anything other than an Italian and his voice stroked her nerve endings like a caress.

Her palm was damp with nerves as she clutched the door-handle and turned it.

He was just a man like any other.

She wasn't going to go weak at the knees. She wasn't going to notice anything about him. She was past all that. She was just going to say what needed to be said and then leave.

Ten minutes, she reminded herself. She just had to survive ten minutes and not back down. And then she'd be on the train back to London.

She opened the door and stepped into the room. 'Hello, Marco.' Her heart fluttered like the wings of a captive butterfly as she forced herself to look at him. 'I wanted to have a quick word before you start surgery.'

His dark eyes met hers and heat erupted through her body, swift and deadly as a forest fire. From throat to pelvis she burned, her reaction to him as powerful as ever. Helplessly, she dug her fingers into her palms.

A man like any other? Had she really believed that, even for a moment? Marco was nothing like any other man.

She'd had two years to prepare herself for this moment, so why did the sight of him drive the last of her breath from her body? What was it about him? Yes, he was handsome but other men were handsome and she barely noticed them. Marco was different. Marco was the embodiment of everything it was to be male. He was strong, confident and unashamedly macho and no woman with a pulse could look at him and not want him.

And for a while he'd been hers.

She looked at him now, unable to think of anything but the hungry, all-consuming passion that had devoured them both.

His powerful body was ominously still, but he said nothing. He simply leaned slowly back in his chair and watched her in brooding silence, his long fingers toying with the pen that he'd been using when she'd entered the room.

Desperately unsettled, Amy sensed the slow simmer of emotion that lay beneath his neutral expression.

What wouldn't she have given to possess even a tiny fraction of his cool?

'We need to talk to each other.' She stayed in the doorway, her hands clasped nervously in front of her, a shiver passing through her body as the atmosphere in the room suddenly turned icy cold.

Finally he spoke. 'You have chosen an odd time of day for a reunion.'

'This isn't a reunion. We have things to discuss, you know we do.'

His gaze didn't flicker. 'And I have thirty sick patients to see before lunchtime. You shouldn't need to ask where my priorities lie.'

No, she didn't need to ask. His skill and dedication as a doctor was one of the qualities that had attracted her to him in the first place.

His handsome face was hard and unforgiving and she felt her insides sink with misery.

What had she expected?

He was hardly going to greet her warmly, was he? Not after the way she'd treated him. *Not after the things she'd let him think about her.* 'I didn't have any choice but to come and see you, Marco. You didn't answer my letters.'

'I didn't like the subject matter.' There was no missing the hard edge to his tone. 'Write about something that interests me and I'll consider replying. And now you need to leave because my first patient is waiting.'

'No.' Panic slid through her and she took a little step forward. 'We need to do this. I know you're upset, but—'

'Upset?' One dark eyebrow rose in sardonic appraisal. 'Why would you possibly think that?'

Her breathing was rapid. 'Please, don't play games—it isn't going to help either of us. Yes, I left, but it was the right thing to do, Marco. It was the right thing for both of us. I'm sure you can understand that now that some time has passed.'

'I understand that you walked out on our marriage. You think "upset"…' his accent thickened as he lingered on the word. 'You think "upset" is an accurate description of my feelings on this subject?'

Amy felt the colour touch her cheeks. The truth was that she had absolutely no insight into his feelings. She'd never really known what he had truly been feeling at any point in their relationship and she hadn't been around to witness his reaction to her departure. If he had been upset then she assumed that it would have been because she'd exposed him to the gossip of a small community, or possibly because he'd had a life plan and she'd ruined it. Not because he'd loved her, because she knew that had never been the case. How could he have loved her? What had she ever been able to offer a man like Marco Avanti?

Especially not once she'd discovered—

Unable to cope with that particular thought at the moment, Amy lifted her chin and ploughed on. 'I can see that you're angry and I don't blame you, but I didn't come here to argue. We can make this easy or we can make it difficult.'

'And I'm sure you're choosing easy.' The contempt in his tone stung like vinegar on an open wound. 'You chose to walk away rather than sort out a problem. Isn't that what you're good at?'

'Not every problem has a solution, Marco!' Frustrated and realising that if she wasn't careful she risked revealing more than she wanted to reveal, she moved closer to the desk. 'You have every right to be upset, but what we need now is to sort out the future. I just need you to agree to the divorce. Then you'll be free to…' *Marry another woman?* The words stuck in her throat.

'*Accidenti*, am I right in understanding that you have interrupted my morning surgery to *ask me for a divorce*?' He rose to his feet, his temper bubbling to the surface, a dangerous glint in his molten dark eyes. 'It is bad enough that I am expected to diagnose a multitude of potentially serious illnesses in a five-minute consultation, but now my wife decides that that in that same ridiculous time frame we are going to end our relationship. This is your idea of a joke, no?'

She'd forgotten how tall he was, how imposing. He topped six feet two and his shoulders were broad and powerful. Looking at him now, she had to force herself not to retreat to the safety of Reception. 'It's not a joke and if I'm interrupting your surgery, it's your fault. You wouldn't answer my letters. I had no other way of getting in touch with you. And this needn't take long.'

He gripped the edge of the desk and his knuckles whitened. 'Do you really think you can leave without explanation and then walk back in here and end our marriage with a five-minute conversation?' His eyes blazed with anger and his voice rose. *'Is that what you think?'*

Startled by his unexpected loss of control, Amy flinched. *She hadn't thought he'd cared so much.*

Caroline Anderson

QUESTIONS & ANSWERS

Would you like to live in the fictional Cornish town of Penhally Bay?

Yes and no. They're interesting people, lots of fascinating stories and interconnected lives, but they're deeply curious about other people's lives and it would be like living in a goldfish bowl! Albeit a very caring one…!

Did you enjoy writing as part of the Brides of Penhally Bay series?

Again, yes and no! It was hard because I couldn't just change things as I went along, which is how I usually work, and yet easier because there was a framework already set out so I didn't have to think about that, just concentrate on making my characters play their parts. I often write linked books so that aspect was second nature to me.

What was it like working with other authors to create the backdrop to these books?

It was a great challenge, and co-ordinating our ideas and characters because they were so intertwined and interconnected was fascinating and would have been impossible without e-mail. It made it harder, because we had to be true to each other's ideas as well as our own. But working with the others was a privilege and I think we all learned a lot.

Tell us about a typical day's writing!

My day starts at six-thirty or so when my husband – if I'm lucky! – brings me a cup of tea in bed. He leaves at seven-ish, and I get up a little while later, have breakfast and walk the dogs, feed the horse and the chickens and then down to the study. Check e-mail, read through the previous day's work, edit, get to the end of what I've written and grind to a halt. Phone a friend! Try again. Go for coffee with friend. Try again. If I'm lucky, it works. If not, walk dogs, think, try again. Dog-walking is great. Empties the mind of everything except the book, and I get fabulous ideas. Then have to race back to the computer and get it all down before it all vanishes into the ether! And once it's going, I tend to write up a storm and finish the book in days. It's getting to that point that's hard, but once there, it just takes over.

How did you first start writing romance novels?

I'd always had a fertile imagination and done bits of creative writing at school and college. I was looking for a change, wanted something that earned a living but was more for *me* that anything I'd done up to then. I'd read lots of Mills & Boon books when my first daughter was tiny, and I thought, why not? So I had a go – well, five, actually, before they accepted me, and since then I've just kept going. This book is number seventy-three, so I suppose I must have got something right!

What do you love most about your hero and heroine in *Christmas Eve Baby*?

Their constancy, and their consideration of the feelings of the others involved in spite of them not always being very reasonable in return! Their determination that their love will endure despite everything in its way, and Ben's protectiveness, both of Lucy and his baby.

Can we have a sneak preview of your next book...?

Of course! It's a Romance, out in the early summer, and it's called *His Pregnant Housekeeper*. And I love it! It's the third book I've set in the fictional Suffolk town of Yoxburgh, which is a blend of Felixstowe, Aldeburgh and Southwold, for those that know the area, and the characters are all heavily involved with each other's lives. Bit like Penhally, really, and just as claustrophobic on occasions!!